DEER IN THE ROAD

CLAUDETTE SABBAG

For my mother, Bette Comet,
who taught me to love books

For my children, Nicholas and Marielle

And for the deer

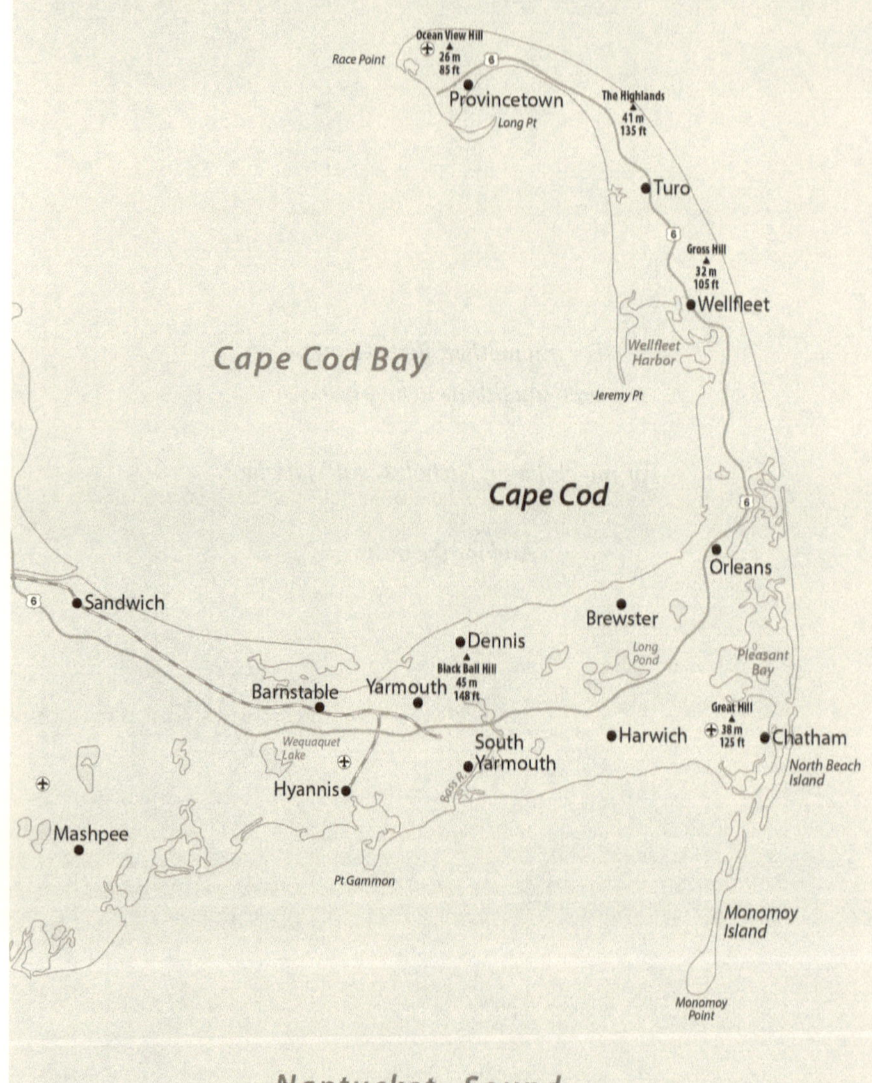

Ocean View Hill
26 m
85 ft
Race Point
6
The Highlands
41 m
135 ft
Provincetown
Long Pt
Turo
6
Gross Hill
32 m
105 ft
Wellfleet
Wellfleet Harbor
Cape Cod Bay
Jeremy Pt
Cape Cod
6
Orleans
Sandwich
6
Brewster
Dennis
Long Pond
Pleasant Bay
Black Ball Hill
45 m
148 ft
Barnstable
Yarmouth
Great Hill
38 m
125 ft
Harwich
Chatham
South Yarmouth
Wequaquet Lake
North Beach Island
Bass R.
Hyannis
Mashpee
Pt Gammon
Monomoy Island
Nantucket Sound
Monomoy Point
Bluffs
Edgartown Bay
Cape Poge
gartown
Sampson Hill
28 m
92 ft
Wasque Point

1

SATURDAY, JUNE 22, 2047

I park at the charging station and glance in the rearview mirror. Running my hands through my tangled curls, I practice a smile. My eyes are somewhat bloodshot; otherwise, my face passes inspection. I gulp down the last drops of the large bottle of electrolyte juice I've nursed on the ride from Boston to tame today's hangover. A little lipstick makes me as ready as I'll ever be. Exiting the car, I smooth down my Cape Rocks Emporium tee shirt, worn in honor of my grandfather's business.

I plug in the car to charge. The saltiness of the sea air fills my lungs as I take three deep, healing breaths. I gaze out over Cape Cod Bay. It shimmers in the sunlight of a cloudless day. An old wooden sailboat progresses slowly across the bay. Electric boats hum past a diesel-powered fishing boat encircled by a flock of seagulls screeching for their share of the catch. A couple of kids run along the water's edge, splashing and laughing, joyful on this first full day of summer.

I wish I felt more joyful on this beautiful day, but my troubled mind won't let me. Another long glance over the water reminds me how much I love every inch of this narrow piece of land that juts into the Atlantic Ocean like a flexed arm: from Hyannis, where solar-powered ferries speed to Martha's Vineyard and Nantucket, to the elbow of Chatham, to the clenched fist of Provincetown, and back down the bay side to the shoulder, where I stand. Sandwich, the oldest European-settled town on Cape Cod, has been my family's home base for many years, but we're in danger of losing it.

Part of the danger comes from the Cape's worst enemy, erosion. The beach below the parking lot has shrunk noticeably since last summer. A narrow strip of sand is all that remains between the waves lapping at the shoreline and the protective wall that extends along the edge of the property. Although scientists and ecologists are racing against time to find ways to prevent the arm of Cape Cod from disappearing, Mother Nature is a tough lady to fight.

I hoist my tote bag on my shoulder and steel myself for this visit with my grandfather, who I love even more than this slim strip of land. The man and the place are inseparable in my mind. As nature and time diminish the land he cherishes, they weaken the man I love. At ninety, he should still live in his beloved house by the sea, strumming his guitar, writing songs, reading, and enjoying the scenery. Unfortunately, my grandmother's death five years ago hit him hard, and the stroke he suffered last year was another massive blow. Now, the cost of this elder home adds to the danger of losing his house.

I make my way into the Sands of the Cape Elder Home, which resembles a cozy Cape Cod inn, with its welcoming lobby and friendly staff who show visitors to the correct room. Although one of the best of its kind, it saddens me that circumstances have forced Grandpa to live here, surrounded by people in worse shape than he is. As I walk down the hall, a man stares vacantly from a wheelchair. A scrawny old woman in a nightgown leans on a walker beside him, engaged in a confused conversation with herself.

Fighting the stress, sadness, and anxiety that return as I think about my grandfather, his house, and my own problems, I pause to collect myself before entering his room. I put a smile on and open the door.

"Hello, Grandpa!"

He sits in his wheelchair in front of a large window, looking out over the bay—the same view from the bedroom of his house, just a few miles up the coast.

"Luna, my little moon rock!" he calls out. Slowly, he opens his arms to hug me.

I bend down into his arms and give him the best hug possible. How small I used to feel next to his almost six-foot height. Now, my five-foot-four-inch frame towers over his wheelchair. When I release him, tears brim in his eyes.

"I'm so happy to see you," he says in a quavering voice.

"I'm happy to see you too." I take his slightly trembling hands in mine and study his face. Despite the deep lines and wrinkles that time, the sun and the wind have etched there, it is still a handsome face with a strong chin, high forehead, and straight nose. His once clear, tawny-brown eyes are faded and cloudy, and his rich, dark-auburn hair has turned white but is still all there, in a shaggy mane around his head.

"How was your trip down this morning? Was there a lot of traffic?"

"It took about an hour and a half—not too bad for a Saturday morning."

"You have an electric car now, I think you told me?"

"Almost all cars are electric now, Grandpa."

"That's good—much better for the environment. But I'd miss that roaring sound of the engine revving up," he says with a little chuckle. "These electric cars are too quiet." He turns his head to look out the window and adds wistfully, "I miss driving."

Now, Grandpa slumps in his wheelchair, still in front of the window. I had encouraged him to go outside to the patio for lunch, but he refused, saying he could see just as well from here. By the time lunch was served and cleared away, he had lost focus, and conversation came to a standstill.

His head falls uncomfortably forward onto his chest. I walk over and quietly say, "It's okay, Grandpa. Take a little nap." I adjust his chair into a reclining position. He falls quickly into a fitful sleep, and I sit watching him, thinking again how sad it is that a man so full of life for so many years has lost his spark.

A warm breeze drifts through the partially open window, carrying the salty smell and soothing sound of the surf gently breaking on the shoreline. Although *soothing* is not the right word for that sound since the surf sneaks a couple of inches closer to the building each year, leaving less and less sand between the Sands of the Cape Elder Home and the sea. The Red Sox game plays on the 3D TV in the corner, the volume turned low, emitting a quiet hum of familiar baseball chatter. I relax in a soft, cushioned chair beside Grandpa and feel sleepy myself, even though it's only one-thirty in the afternoon. This is going to be one long day.

Maybe I should take a nap. I stayed up much too late last night. I declined an invitation to a Summer Solstice party, claiming I needed a good night's sleep to be fresh for my trip to the Cape. So much for that: I ended up surfing mindlessly through TV channels, alone in my apartment, drinking one too many—or two or three too many—glasses of wine. I close my eyes for a few minutes, but my mind races with thoughts of all that needs to be done before I head back to Boston tomorrow.

Besides visiting Grandpa this weekend, I must check on the condition of his house. Initially, he was financially well off enough to afford the private elder home and still retain possession of his house. But his savings have dwindled, and insurance covers only a small percentage of the expense of the home. So, the family is talking about selling his house. It's shocking to me that they would even consider this, given the many fond memories they share of their home on the beach.

The problem is I'm the only one who lives close enough to use it regularly. My mom and aunt stay there occasionally when they visit Grandpa, but I'm there two or three times a month. The house means so much to me. It has been my happy place since childhood, filled with warm memories of my loving grandparents. Recently, it has become a haven from the city, my job, and my apartment, which I'm also likely to lose since Rafael moved out last year, leaving me with all the bills.

I must convince the family to rent rather than sell, so I've tasked myself with assessing its condition and listing any major work it needs. I have to move swiftly since mid-July is only a few weeks away—already a little late for the start of the prime summer rental season on the Cape. If renting will pay the way, the family might reconsider. The fact that Grandpa doesn't know about any of this yet adds to my stress.

Grandpa snorts in his sleep, bringing me back to the present. I don't know what to do with myself. Part of me wants to read or write something. I have brought along the large, colorful, hand-woven tote bag my grandmother made, filled with my old-fashioned notebooks, wood pencils, and print books, but I don't have the energy to focus. I watch the Sox game for a bit. They're winning, which would make Grandpa happy. He's a loyal fan, even though they haven't won a World Series in almost thirty years. Grandpa likes to remind people that the Red Sox once went eighty-six years without winning the Series, so this is nothing.

My device vibrates in my pocket. I glance at the screen as I walk into the hall and read the text from my mother, asking how things are going. I reply positively. I find myself standing in front of my grandfather's memory box, which all the elders have outside their rooms. These large glass cases display photos and memorabilia from each resident's life. Grandpa's name stands out in golden, three-dimensional letters in the center of the box:

Jonathan David Rock

3D images of newspaper clippings and bulletins cycle around his name: Hurricane Bob of 1991, the terrorist attacks of September 11, 2001, the Pandemic of the '20s, the International Peace Treaty of 2040, and other historical events. Posters of Grateful Dead concerts from the 1970s and '80s, promotional brochures advertising the Cape Rocks Emporium and Wampanoag Wares, album covers, sheet music, old baseball cards, and concert tickets pop up here and there. Hand-painted heart rocks, small wooden, carved animals, sea glass figurines, beaded jewelry, and small woven baskets cover the bottom of the box. Photographs of the family also appear in 3D images.

My favorite photo of my grandparents, taken on their wedding day, cycles by. They stand on the beach with the wind whipping through their long, flowing hair. Grandpa's auburn hair glows in the sun, and Grandma's dark chocolate waves intermingle with his as they wrap their arms around each other. He wears lightweight, loose, tan cotton pants with a matching tunic embroidered with multicolored beads in intricate patterns. Her loose, ankle-length dress is of the same material and design. They smile straight into the camera, radiating happiness I cannot help but share all these years later.

The second photo that catches my eye shows my grandparents with their three children twenty years later. It was also taken on the beach, on a cool, windy April day, on my Aunt April's eighteenth birthday. They are dressed in jeans and sweatshirts, sitting on an outcropping of large rocks. Grandpa's hair has lost some of the auburn highlights and has a few strands of gray, but it is still long, tied back in a ponytail. He now sports a short beard and mustache. Grandma's dark-brown hair is mixed with white and falls in two long braids that frame her still-lovely face. Their children sit in front of them: April, her long brown hair fluttering around her strong, smiling face, August, a few years younger, his black shaggy hair blowing into his eyes, and Soleil, their shining little sun, sits on August's lap, her curly, orange hair glowing in a mop around her beaming face. She's my mom, who is less than three years old in this photo.

"I love your grandfather's name," a soft voice says behind me.

I turn to see a tall, dark-skinned, middle-aged woman smiling as she also looks into the memory box. She's one of the home's caregivers I haven't yet met.

"I like to tease him about how funny my name would be if we were married," she adds in her slightly accented English.

I look at her name tag and laugh, "Your name is Amoon? Is that how you say it, *uh moon*?"

"Yes, pretty close. So, if we were married, my name would be *a moon rock*. But I understand you have that name already. Your grandfather talks about you often."

"Well, my name is Luna, which is *moon* in Spanish, and Rock is my middle name. So, you could say my name is Moon Rock, but my last name is Martinez, which takes away from the effect."

Amoon glances back at the memory box, and the 3D photo of my grandparents on their wedding day appears again.

"You have the same coloring as your grandfather when he was young, that beautiful dark reddish brown hair, with eyes the same color."

"Thanks. I'm glad it came out this color instead of my mom's bright orange," I say, pointing out my mom as a photo of her appears. "But that's perfect for her. She is like her name, *the sun*."

"She is beautiful, and your grandfather also speaks of her often. I am happy to meet you, Luna," says Amoon, placing her right hand over her heart.

"Happy to meet you too, Amoon," I reply and return the greeting.

"Is your grandfather sleeping?"

"Yes, he got tired after lunch."

"I will go in and get him up and moving. If he sleeps too much in the day, he is awake at night."

"Thank you. I'll come back in a few minutes."

I RETURN to Grandpa's room after Amoon has checked his vital signs and given him his med injection, which should energize him. He sits in his wheelchair, staring out the window at the sea. The day has warmed considerably, and Amoon has closed the windows to the sounds and scents of the beach beyond.

"Hi, Grandpa. Did you have a nice nap?" I resume my spot in the chair beside him.

"Was I sleeping? I'm sorry."

"Nothing to be sorry about."

"So, what are you doing these days? Have you written your first book yet?"

I roll my eyes in gentle annoyance at this question that gets asked all too often by family and friends. Gathering my patience, I sigh and answer as I always do. "No, but I have many ideas and still keep my notebooks nearby to write them down. One of these days, I'll get an idea for a whole book, but who knows when I'll have time to write it. My job at the publishing company keeps me too busy and tired to do anything of my own."

Four years ago, after graduating college with a degree in creative writing, I started work at Pure Print Publishing. I was impressed that they publish only print books without the help of artificial intelligence. Part of their mission is replanting the trees cut down to produce paper with a reforestation program, ensuring the entire printing process is ecologically clean. Unfortunately, my job consists mainly of tedious clerical work. It doesn't require creative writing skills and doesn't pay enough to cover my monthly expenses.

"If you can't find the time now, while you're young and free, you'll never find it. Don't wait too long. Time goes by way too fast, I can tell you that."

"I won't, Grandpa, I promise," I say soothingly. I put my hand over his and rub it gently.

He closes his eyes, and just as I think he's falling asleep again, he suddenly opens them wide and asks, "Where's the deer? Where's my deer?" His eyes dart around the room, and his hands tighten on the arms of the wheelchair.

"What deer? You must have been dreaming."

"No, my deer, the wooden deer. Where is it? I know it's here somewhere."

I have a vague memory of a carved, wooden deer Grandpa kept in the bedroom of his house. That's another thing we like about this elder home: They encourage families to furnish the rooms with the elders' own possessions to make them feel more at home. I look around the room but see nothing on the bookcase or bedside tables. I go over to the large oak dresser along the side wall, piled with cards and letters, vases of flowers, stuffed animals, and other gifts from friends and family. Sure enough, there's the deer lying on its side behind a carved seagull.

"Here it is. I found it!"

I bring the deer to his shaking outstretched hands. He gently takes it, rubbing its back on a smooth spot that looks like it has seen many such caresses. The carving is about eight by six inches, a perfect fit for his hands. The deer is finely detailed, with perfect, three-pointed antlers and realistic glass eyes that glint in the sunlight streaming through the window.

"Did Grandma's brother carve that deer?" I remember he'd been a woodcarver who had taught my Uncle August his trade.

"Yes, Willy carved this deer. You didn't know him, did you?"

"No, but I've heard stories about him."

"You know about the deer, don't you? I've told you about that." His eyes brighten as he pushes himself upright in his wheelchair.

"You must have, but I don't remember all of it." I remember some of the story, but this is the most excited he's been all day. It might be good to get him talking. "Tell it to me now, Grandpa," I say to encourage him. "We have plenty of time."

"It happened a long time ago," he starts, then pauses, thinking back. "It was when I was twenty years old. Remind me how old I am now?"

"You're ninety, remember? We had that big party for you back in February?"

"Okay, so this happened seventy years ago. I can't believe how old I am. Anyway, it was Fourth of July weekend of 1977. The Fourth fell on a Monday that year. I like it when the Fourth falls on a Monday…"

2

FRIDAY, JULY 1, 1977

Jonathan plunked some coins into the Coke machine in the Shop n' Save staff room and grabbed that red can of caffeine and sugar to give him the energy for his drive to the Cape. He would be on the road by nine-thirty and, if Cape traffic weren't too bad—a lot to hope for on Friday of Fourth of July weekend—he'd be at Michelle's house before midnight. That would leave enough time for a few beers around the fire pit before crashing for a good night's sleep—an excellent start to a well-deserved long weekend away from work, his house, and his parents.

He headed to the parking lot, calling "Goodbye" and "Have a great weekend!" to his coworkers.

"Bye, Jonathan. Have fun at the Cape. Kiss Michelle for me!" yelled his friend, Mark, laughing his crazy laugh.

"I will, Mark. You have fun, too!"

"Have a nice Fourth, Jonny!" called Gloria, the new girl from the deli. No one had told her he only answered to Jonathan, never Jon or Jonny. Oh well, he'd deal with that later.

"You too, Gloria!" he called back as he opened his car door.

Even though he had owned this car for over two years,

Jonathan never failed to feel excited as he slid into the driver's seat of the '71 dark-green Ford Mustang. He kept it immaculately clean, inside and out. His friends and family made fun of him about that. Jonathan could never figure out what was wrong with keeping his things looking good. Then again, he usually thought differently from other people.

Jonathan turned the key, revved the engine, backed out, and started his weekend. He had promised himself to relax and not think about everything bothering him. He would ignore all those voices in his head, primarily his father's, constantly lecturing him about how he should live his life.

The fact that Jonathan had given in and gone to Bancroft Business College and majored in marketing instead of the Newbury School of Music should have made his father happy. But no, his father criticized him constantly: Jonathan's hair was too long, he looked like a hippie, he should be looking for an entry-level job in the business world instead of wasting his time cashiering at the Shop 'n Save, and he definitely should not be going to Grateful Dead concerts with those weirdos. That Jonathan had written almost an entire album of songs did nothing to impress his father.

All Jonathan wanted was to be himself. Why did that have to be so hard?

"Stop!" he yelled out loud. *Stop going over all this crap again and again! This weekend is to relax, let it go, and just have fun for a change.* He turned up the volume on the radio. Jimmy Buffet was singing "Margaritaville." *I wish I were in Margaritaville.* He sipped his Coke and relaxed into the ride.

It was a long one, with pockets of traffic converging off and on between Boston and the Sagamore Bridge. He crossed over the Cape Cod Canal at half-past eleven. He should arrive at Michelle's house by midnight. Knowing her, she'd probably complain about how late he was, no matter when he arrived.

Michelle was another subject those voices in his head kept

yammering about. She had changed significantly over this last year, her first and Jonathan's second in college. Their interests in music, movies, and even food were drifting further and further apart. Last year, she happily accompanied him to not one but two Grateful Dead concerts. Last month, she tried to get him to go to a disco, which he despised! Maybe this weekend would be the final test of their relationship.

The Allman Brothers sang "Ramblin Man" on the radio. Jonathan turned it up. He concentrated on the road, driving as fast as he could without exceeding the speed limit too much. He stayed in the fast lane as long as there was one to avoid the slowpokes, although few cars were on the road now.

Suddenly, a large, dark shape emerged from the right side of the road. Before his mind could take it in, a deer stood directly in front of the car. He slammed on the brakes, but even as he did so, he had a split-second to take in the beauty of the animal before him. It was a young buck, its head with two three-pointed antlers held high. Its dark eyes, shining in the moonlight, stared straight at him.

There was no way he could stop in time. He hit the deer full-on. It bounced off the front hood, hit the windshield, and rolled over the car's roof, landing on the gravel shoulder behind him. The steering wheel rammed into his chest. The windshield fractured into a mosaic of granular glass but didn't break in.

Shaken, Jonathan pulled the car off the pavement onto the left shoulder. He sat there momentarily, the breath knocked out of him, trying to get his lungs to work. It occurred to him to put on the four-way flashers. He opened the door but couldn't get out; his seat belt was still buckled. He released it and crawled out, straightening up painfully.

He quivered from head to toe. His knees threatened to give way, so he leaned against the car for support.

He crept unsteadily to the back of the car, where the

bulky shape of the mangled deer lay. He watched for any sign of life, but it was motionless. The deer lay on its side, legs and neck splayed at odd angles. The full moon and the glow from his flashing hazard lights were enough to show Jonathan that the deer's eyes were still open, fixed blindly on the night sky. A dark patch of blood covered its side, pooling into the ground.

A pickup truck pulled over about twenty feet behind him. Its headlights threw the body of the deer into relief, bringing to light the red of the blood and the gash on its side. After a moment, a figure emerged, shining a flashlight. At first, Jonathan thought it was a man in baggy jeans, a loose tee shirt, and a baseball cap, but a woman's voice called out to him.

"Are you okay?"

"I think so," Jonathan replied shakily. The act of speaking brought him close to tears.

The woman pointed her flashlight at the body. "That's a big deer you hit. You're lucky you weren't killed!" She directed the flashlight toward his car. "It looks like maybe your car was, though."

Jonathan staggered back to his Mustang. The car was in worse shape than he had imagined. The front, the hood, and the roof were all badly crushed, along with the shattered windshield. His heart ached as much for his car as for his bruised chest.

"Are you sure you're okay?" she repeated.

Jonathan stretched tentatively. "My chest hurts where I hit the steering wheel," he admitted, "but I don't think it's anything serious. I'm pretty shaky, but I think I'm alright."

"You're lucky, that's for sure," said the woman. "I contacted the police on my CB. They should be here soon."

"Thanks," said Jonathan.

A siren sounded in the distance.

A few minutes later, the police arrived, followed by a tow

truck. The truck would tow Jonathan's car to a nearby service station and take the deer to wherever they took dead deer.

"That's a handsome buck," the tow truck driver said. He picked up the deer's head by the antlers. "Unusual for a buck to have such clean points this time of year. He's still got enough undamaged meat on him for someone to enjoy a good venison meal this weekend."

The idea of reducing the deer into impersonal portions of meat sickened Jonathan. He didn't want to think about that. He kept seeing the deer's eyes staring at him in the seconds before he hit it.

He convinced the police officer that he didn't need to go to the hospital and that he had friends nearby. The woman with the pickup truck would drive him there. He retrieved his duffel bag and guitar from the backseat of the car, put the slip of paper with the name and number of the service station where his car was being towed into the pocket of his jeans, and climbed into the pickup.

"Thank you so much for giving me a ride," Jonathan said, his voice steadier now.

"No problem," said the woman. "I'm on my way to Province-town, so everything between here and there is on the way. By the way, my name is Diane."

"Nice to meet you, Diane. I'm Jonathan."

"Nice to meet you, Jonathan. I'm glad to help. You've had a rough night."

DIANE LEFT Jonathan in front of Michelle's house a little after twelve-thirty. Michelle would probably be annoyed he was late, but at this point, he didn't care about anything except having a beer or two to relax his aching body and crawling into bed. He hoisted his duffel bag on one shoulder and his guitar on the other and headed toward the front door. The traditional party around the fire pit was probably over. Then, he heard laughter from the backyard. Instead of knocking and disturbing Michelle's parents and the dog, Jonathan walked around the side of the large, sprawling house. Sure enough, a small fire still crackled, and a few young people sat around it, speaking in low voices.

Michelle spotted Jonathan and ran toward him, "Jonathan! You're here!" She threw her arms around him. He winced. "What took you so long? Was traffic bad?"

"No, I was in an accident. I hit a deer. It wrecked my car."

"Oh no! Are you okay?"

"My chest hurts like hell from hitting the steering wheel. But otherwise, I'm in one piece."

"What about your car?"

"They had to tow it away. It's probably totaled."

She asked question after question. He gave her the essential details.

Michelle's guests called from near the fire pit, "Hey, what are you guys doing? Come over to the fire. Hi Jonathan, what's happening?"

Jonathan knew Michelle's friends from previous Cape trips —Amy and Judy, and Judy's boyfriend, Danny. He didn't feel talkative or sociable, but Michelle took his hand and led him to the fire. "Jonathan hit a deer and wrecked his car on the way here. I think he needs a beer."

At this point, there were more questions and more beers. At least one joint made the rounds. He accepted the offerings and wearily explained what had happened. More to soothe himself than to entertain the group, Jonathan eventually picked up his guitar and strummed some quiet tunes until everyone stopped talking and listened to the music.

The curfew Michelle's parents had set for the end of the party had long since passed when her father flicked the back porch light on and off several times, the signal to come in. They doused the fire with the hose and went inside to their various beds. Michelle's house was more than big enough to accommodate her four guests. Jonathan admired the house, but it stood in the middle of the Cape. They had to drive to get to either the ocean or the bay. *What's the point of having a house on the Cape that isn't on the water?* Jonathan thought. *If I'm ever lucky enough to own a house on Cape Cod, it will be right on the beach.*

Jonathan and Michelle sat together in the kitchen after the others had gone to bed. He had stowed his bag and guitar in Mr. Armont's office, where he would sleep on a couch that Mrs. Armont had neatly made up with sheets and blankets. Michelle pulled out a bottle of Jack Daniels and offered him a shot.

"Okay, but just one," Jonathan said. "I am so exhausted."

"Oh, well," Michelle huffed. "That's a great way to start the weekend." She poured them each a double shot. "You've been a real joy so far. You acted like you didn't want to talk to anyone tonight."

Jonathan took a swallow of the drink and stared at her.

Here it comes again, he thought. She had developed a sarcastic attitude over the past year. Her freshman year of college had taught her nothing but how to be nasty-tempered. *What happened to the easy-going girl I dated in high school?*

"Are you kidding?" he asked her. "Did you not understand that I was just in a bad accident? I was almost killed. I would have been if that deer had come through the windshield!" Jonathan's voice trembled as he spoke slowly, hunting for words to describe his feelings. He realized that he was still shivering internally. *This must be what they call shock.* "Not to mention the fact that I killed the deer. I can still see its eyes staring at me before I hit it."

"Oh my god, it was just a deer. There are too many of them around here. That's why they're always getting hit by cars. Are you going to cry about it?"

That did it. Jonathan swigged down the rest of his drink and carefully placed the glass on the table, fighting the impulse to slam it down or, better yet, hurl it at Michelle's head. He walked down the hall to his room. As he crawled under the blanket, grateful for the soft warmth around his sore, tired body, he wished he had gone to bed sooner.

I need to get a new life, he thought as he closed his aching eyes, *but how?*

3

SATURDAY, JULY 2, 1977

Jonathan awoke to a light tapping. He opened his eyes and looked around, confused about where he was.

"Jonathan, are you awake?" came Michelle's timid voice from the other side of the door. "Can I come in?"

The events of last night tumbled back into his brain: the drive to the Cape, the deer, the woman with the pickup, the fire pit, Michelle. Jonathan sat up and ran his hands through his long, auburn hair. He felt like he'd been hit by a truck. Every muscle and joint throbbed. The collision with the deer had jolted his body more than he realized. Plus, he had a pounding headache, brought on by the double shot of Jack Daniels right before bed, on top of the beers and hits of weed.

"Sure, come in." What else could he say? He certainly didn't feel like arguing now.

Michelle slowly opened the door and came in. She walked over to the couch, sat beside him, and gently put her arms around him. Her long blond hair intermingled with his.

"I am so sorry," she said in a shaky voice. "I get to be such a bitch sometimes when I drink. I'm sorry about the deer and your car. I just wanted this to be a fun weekend."

Jonathan returned her hug. "So did I, Michelle. But I sometimes don't know who you are anymore." He shifted to get out of the blankets. "I don't want to talk about it now. What time is it?"

"It's nine o'clock. My mom's got breakfast ready. Then we're going to the flea market in Sandwich, and we want to get there early before all the good stuff is gone."

Jonathan had assumed they would hang out at the beach all day, but Michelle said they would do that after the flea market. The aroma drifting from the kitchen enticed him to get up. He had not eaten anything since a piece of pizza on his afternoon break the day before. Mrs. Armont's legendary breakfast would go far to ease his aches and pains, as well as his appetite.

After washing up and consuming a large amount of waffles, sausages, scrambled eggs, coffee, and orange juice, Jonathan was on the mend. Before they left, he called his parents to tell them about the deer. As he dialed his home number, he mentally prepared himself for his father's nagging advice about driving more carefully. In his father's opinion, the accident was sure to be his fault, not the deer's.

"First of all, are you okay?" Jonathan's father asked.

"I feel sore and achy, but I'm okay."

"It's a good thing you were wearing your seatbelt."

"Of course, I always wear it." That was another thing Jonathan's friends teased him about, but this time, he was grateful for having followed his own good sense.

"How fast were you going? Were you paying attention to the road or singing along to some song on the radio?"

"I was going about sixty, and yes, I was paying close attention. The radio had nothing to do with it. The deer came out of nowhere. It's dark on that part of the road. There was no way to avoid it."

The conversation ended with his dad taking the number of the service station that towed the car. He said he would *take*

care of it, implying that Jonathan wasn't capable of doing so. *Fine by me,* Jonathan thought as he hung up the phone.

MRS. ARMONT DROVE them to the flea market in her huge Woodie station wagon. Jonathan's mom had one that was almost the same. Michelle and Amy sat up front, chatting and giggling. Jonathan sat in the back with Judy and Danny, who had their arms around each other's shoulders, whispering. Content to be left alone, Jonathan watched the passing Cape Cod scenery: cozy gray cottages, souvenir shops, candy stores, ice cream and beach plum jam stands, seafood restaurants, and intermittent glimpses of the ocean as they got closer to Sandwich. Even in the tourist-infested summer season, Cape Cod's ambiance was a balm for Jonathan's soul, and by the time they arrived at the flea market, he felt much better.

They pulled into the flea market at eleven, parking in a grassy field. The market consisted of three rows of stalls running about a football field in length. The group started out together but became separated as some took longer than others at display tables and booths. A wide variety of items crowded each stall: second-hand and new jewelry, antique furniture, old records and books, paintings, posters, handmade soaps, candles, pottery, and a lot of just plain old junk. Food and drink stands enticed passersby with the scent of hotdogs, hamburgers, fried dough, and pizza, and the refreshing sound of drinks splashing over ice cubes.

Within half an hour, Jonathan had purposely lost himself from the others. A lemonade stand caught his eye toward the end of the third row. He stopped for a large one, made to order by a pretty teenage girl. She smiled at him and asked if he'd like extra ice. He was parched, and the drink went down too fast, giving him a brain freeze. It was just what he needed, however, to re-energize. The hot day was not ideal for wandering around a dry, treeless field under the midday sun.

Jonathan decided to finish browsing this row, then find a shady spot to sit and wait for Michelle to find him.

The last stall stood on the left side, a bit removed from the others, in front of an old, green-and-white VW Microbus. No one was outside watching over the display as Jonathan walked over to inspect its items. The table was covered with woven cloth bags and baskets of various sizes, beaded jewelry, carved wooden figures of animals, painted heart-shaped rocks, and small birds, fish, and turtles made from sea glass.

Jonathan took his time looking over everything. Each item appeared to be handmade and of a higher quality than anything else he had seen at the flea market. In the center of the table, a small, handprinted sign leaned against a carved wooden bear, with the words *Wampanoag Wares* painted in rainbow-colored letters.

As he continued inspecting the objects on the table, his gaze fell upon a carved wooden deer, a buck with three-pointed antlers standing with its head turned to the left. It stared at him with shining, dark eyes. A wave of shock ran down his spine, transporting him to the night before, his foot stomping on the brake in that moment before impact. This deer was a perfect replica of the live one he had killed. The memory weighed heavily on his mind.

Jonathan picked up the deer for closer inspection. A young woman appeared at the bus's open side door, stepped down, and came to the table. She was about his age, with long, straight, dark hair that flowed down the sides of her tanned face. The girl had a distinctive appearance, pretty but strong, with a prominent nose and large dark-brown eyes. She watched him with interest. She wore a loose-fitting, white cotton dress with patterns of multi-colored beads around the top. She smiled. Her top front teeth were a little crooked, one slightly in front of the other.

"You like the deer?" she asked. "My brother made it. He carved all of these animals," she said proudly. Her voice was soft, deep, and rich.

"Yes, it reminds me of another deer I saw recently," Jonathan responded. "How much is it?"

"It's twenty dollars," she answered. "It is hand-carved. My brother takes a long time to complete his carvings. Notice the small details, all the fine lines to look like real fur and the realistic eyes."

The life-like quality of the deer had caught Jonathan's eye. He took his wallet from his back pocket. He had about eighty dollars in cash, so there would be plenty to buy dinner and drinks for Michelle at the Lobster Claw. Even if it weren't enough, Michelle always had money.

He knew buyers were supposed to argue over prices at flea markets, but he hated doing that. His father was a big haggler who tried to instill in him the rule of never paying the original asking price, but Jonathan found that uncomfortable and embarrassing. Besides, there was something about this girl he liked. She seemed so different from Michelle and her friends. She had a calm, self-assured manner and was beautiful in a unique way.

He handed a twenty-dollar bill to her. "Here you go," he said. "Thank you." He picked up the deer again and stroked its back in a gesture that would be repeated thousands of times in the future.

"Oh, thank you!" the girl answered. She smiled more broadly now, and her whole face lit up. Somehow, those slightly crooked teeth made her face even more perfect. "I hope you enjoy it for many years."

"I will," he answered, surprised at how fervently he felt that.

He wished he could think of something else to say. Before he could, Michelle and Amy caught up with him.

"There you are! We've been looking all over for you," said Michelle. "My mom wants to leave so we can get to the beach. It's so hot!"

"Well, I'm right here," he said. He cast a tentative smile at the girl before walking away with Michelle. "Look, I found this carving of a deer. It looks just like the one I hit last night. I think it's a sign that I should have it."

"Nice," Michelle said without enthusiasm. "How much was it?".

"Twenty dollars. It's handmade."

"Wow, that's a lot," Amy said.

"That is a lot of money for some cheap Indian knick-knack," Michelle said, looking over to where the dark-haired girl talked with another customer.

"You know what, Michelle?" Jonathan said, trying to keep an edge off his voice. "Let's just not talk about it, okay?"

"Yeah, let's go to the beach!" Amy said. She and Michelle hooked arms and walked off ahead of him. Jonathan followed them to the parking lot.

"That's a beautiful carving, Jonathan," Mrs Armont said.

"Thanks," Jonathan said, glancing at Michelle, who shrugged her shoulders and got into the car.

On the ride home, Michelle and Amy chatted with Mrs. Armont about their purchases. Judy and Danny resumed their cuddling and whispering in the back seat. Jonathan sat beside them, looking out the window, stroking the deer's back. Jonathan didn't speak to Michelle or the others until after they had returned to the house, changed, and gathered their beach things.

As they headed back out, Michelle broke the silence. "So, are you not going to speak to me for the rest of the weekend?

I'm sorry about what I said about the deer, but I don't think you should have paid that much for it."

"Okay, Michelle, I hear you, but that's your opinion." He huffed. "I'm having a hard time talking to you about anything anymore."

The truth was that if he had wheels, Jonathan would have packed his things and left right then and there. The more he thought about it, the more he realized how far apart he and Michelle had grown. In fact, he wasn't sure they had ever been that close. With no way to get home, however, he felt trapped in the situation.

"What does that mean?" she asked in her snarky way. "Are you breaking up with me in the middle of Fourth of July weekend?"

"I don't know. At this point, it seems like I can't say or do anything right."

Jonathan felt like an idiot. *Why can't I just say what I feel?* He was always afraid of causing problems, whether with his parents, friends, or Michelle. Now that he thought of it, why should it matter that he didn't have a car? He loved stories about people who just took off down the road and walked or hitchhiked to wherever the wind blew them. *Why can't I do that? I'm such a wimp.*

Michelle put her arms around him. In an apologetic tone, she said, "Well, I say we put some vodka in the cranberry juice, go to the beach, and chill."

Jonathan hugged her, resigned at least to the day. Maybe time at the beach would help calm them both. "Okay, let's go."

THE REST of the day was a blur of drinks on the beach, dinner at the Lobster Claw, and sitting around the fire pit at Michelle's house

that night. The alcohol helped to mellow them all for a while. Jonathan played his guitar off and on throughout the day and evening. That always calmed him. Still, he could not completely let go of the tension that he felt between himself and Michelle.

The tension reared its head again around midnight, when the fire was dying, and everyone was too tired to start it again. Michelle led Jonathan away from the others and asked if he wanted to go down to the basement bedroom, known for its out-of-earshot location. They had used it on several occasions for a quick tumble.

"Sorry, but I'm exhausted. I'm going to head to bed."

"You haven't been any fun this weekend," Michelle said, annoyed. "What's with you?"

"I feel like we aren't on the same wavelength. We seem to irritate each other more than anything else."

Michelle crossed her arms and lifted her chin, her blue eyes blazing. "Well, maybe this isn't working anymore."

"I'm beginning to think that, too," he said. "I'm sorry, Michelle. Good night." He turned and walked into the house.

She didn't follow him but returned to the fire. A few minutes later, he heard her laughing with her friends.

Jonathan went into his room and packed his duffle bag. He carefully wrapped the wooden deer in a tee shirt to protect it. After placing his sandals on top of the bag, Jonathan went over to Mr. Armont's desk, found a blank piece of paper, grabbed a pen, and wrote Michelle a note:

Michelle - You're right - it's not working - Sorry - Jonathan

He left the note in the middle of the desk and lay down on the couch on top of the blankets. He would sleep for a few hours, get up before dawn, and hit the road with his duffel bag and guitar.

It was time to stop thinking about making changes. It was time for action.

4

____

SUNDAY, JULY 3, 1977

Jonathan woke shortly before five after a fitful sleep. He stretched, relieved that his body's soreness of the previous day had diminished. He grabbed his duffel bag and guitar and tiptoed slowly out of the house, sandals in hand. He prayed that Michelle's dog, Sandy, a large Golden Retriever, wouldn't hear him and start barking, but either she was sound asleep or getting deaf in her old age. She didn't make a sound.

As Jonathan walked across the front lawn, the morning dew wet on his feet, he felt a new sense of freedom and happiness. He stopped at the edge of the road to put on his sandals. The sun lit the eastern sky with an orange-pink glow. With the sandy, seashell-strewn Cape road under his feet and a firm resolve in his heart, Jonathan was confident that he was embarking on a new phase of his life.

He walked steadily and easily in the dawning day, past still-sleeping Cape houses and closed shops. It was a perfect summer morning: the sun was warm, and the air was fresh and clear. When he got to Route 6A, he headed west toward Sandwich and the Sagamore Bridge. Eventually, he would have to hitchhike unless he found a Boston-bound bus. The idea of hitchhiking made him nervous, but it was something he needed to do if he were to become the carefree adventurer he admired in books like *On The Road*.

Jonathan kept a steady pace for almost two hours. Hungry, he stopped at a small cafe for coffee and a muffin. He figured he had walked about six miles, but quite a few more lay between him and the bridge. Maybe it was time to look for a ride. He crossed the road to a gas station to ask people heading west if they could give him a ride. His Jack Kerouac blood wasn't flowing strong enough yet to give him the courage to stick his thumb out, but he was determined to hitchhike before the day ended.

At the station, only a few cars waited in line for gas, and fewer were parked at the small convenience store. It was Sunday of a long Fourth of July weekend; most people would stay until Monday or Tuesday, if not for the entire week, but he'd try his luck. A young guy with long hair and a tie-dye shirt came out of the store with a coffee, heading toward a battered old Chevy. Jonathan approached him with a wave of his hand.

"Hey man, how you doing? I'm heading off the Cape and need a ride. Would you be going that way?"

"I'm only going as far as Sandwich, but I can drop you off there."

"That's perfect. Thanks!"

Jonathan put his duffel bag and guitar in the back seat of the Chevy and got into the passenger seat. He talked easily with the young man as they continued through the small Cape towns decorated with American flags and red, white, and blue streamers. Many of these streets would soon be closed off to host small-town parades later today or tomorrow.

"My name's Nick," the driver said.

"Nice to meet you. I'm Jonathan."

"Too bad you have to leave the Cape today. The weather's great, and you'll miss the fireworks!"

"Things weren't working out with the people I was staying with, so I decided to head home early."

"I'm staying with some friends in a house on the beach in East Sandwich. There's plenty of room if you need a place to stay. Big party on the beach tonight!"

The offer tempted Jonathan, but he did not feel quite that adventurous yet. As it was, he had enough to deal with at home. He declined the invitation with thanks. Nick dropped him off in downtown Sandwich, only a few miles from the bridge.

By mid-morning, Jonathan got to wondering what was happening at Michelle's house. He was tempted to find a pay phone and call her but talked himself out of it. Maybe he'd call when he got home. He didn't want this to be a nasty breakup, but the high school romance clearly was over. Their interests had grown further apart, and the feelings they once shared for one another had dwindled. He would wish her well and say goodbye.

He should also call his parents, in case Mr. and Mrs. Armont had called them, but decided against that also. He was a twenty-year-old adult who should be able to make his own decisions. He still avoided thinking about the difficult issues that would arise as he followed through on his resolve to live his own life. It would mean leaving Bancroft Business College and dealing with his father's anger. It would also mean moving out of his parent's house. He would have to find a way to make it on his own financially.

The high arch of the Sagamore Bridge became visible in the distance. Once over that, it was still over fifty miles to Boston and another twenty-five to home. Jonathan would either have to walk on the main highway, which wasn't legal, use backroads, find a bus, or embrace his new brave, adventurous self and hitchhike. A few more cars were heading for the bridge, building steadily, but nothing like the bumper-to-bumper traffic that would form at the end of the long weekend.

Now was the time. Jonathan turned to face the bridge-bound cars, slung his duffel bag over his left shoulder and guitar over his right, and stuck out his thumb. He smiled slightly, to look as friendly and nonchalant as possible, and hoped for some hippies to come along.

He counted the cars that drove past to occupy his mind. He had counted thirty-eight when an old VW Microbus slowed down as it approached him. *These have got to be hippies.* The bus crept past him and pulled over. He couldn't see well into the bus, but it looked like there was just the driver. He ran to the passenger-side door and opened it.

The driver was the dark-haired girl from the flea market.

Of course, now I remember this VW bus!

She smiled calmly, her dark brown eyes looking into his. As recognition dawned on his face, her smile widened, showing those two crooked front teeth. That smile made Jonathan unexplainably happy.

"Hi," he said. "You're the girl from the flea market!"

"Yes, I am the girl from the flea market. And you are the boy who bought the deer. And it looks like now you are the boy who needs a ride."

"Yes," he said, mimicking her tone. "That would be me, the boy who bought the deer and who now needs a ride. I'm heading off the Cape toward Boston, so it would be great if you're heading in that direction."

"Hop in," she said, and he did. She pulled back onto the road, and they drove in companionable silence until they were over the bridge and heading north.

"So, where exactly are you going?" she asked. "I have to drop some things off at a store in Plymouth, but I could drive you up to Boston after."

"You're going only as far as Plymouth? Boston is way out of your way! I can catch a bus in Plymouth."

"That's okay. It's early, it's Sunday, and I have nothing else to do."

"Well, that's very nice of you. At least let me pay you for gas."

"Okay," she agreed without arguing, "and you can help me carry boxes into the store in Plymouth."

They soon arrived at a tourist shop in Plymouth, where the girl delivered her craft items. They carried in several boxes of wood carvings, woven blankets, baskets, beaded clothing, jewelry, and painted heart rocks. At a coffee shop next door, Jonathan insisted on treating her to drinks and snacks for the road. He also used the payphone to call his parents and tell them he was coming home early. He didn't mention hitchhiking; he said he was riding with a friend of Michelle's who would take him to North Station, where he could catch a train home.

They talked easily as they drove toward Boston. They swapped names. The girl's name was Winter because she was born on December 21st, the winter solstice. She was a member of the Wampanoag tribe of Native Americans. Jonathan told her about hitting the deer and breaking up with his girlfriend to explain why he was hitching his way home early on the holiday weekend.

"Why are you and your girlfriend breaking up?" Winter asked.

"We met and dated all through high school and had a lot of fun back then. But over the last year, we've gone in different directions. She's developed some heavy-duty sarcasm and is sometimes just plain rude. When I said I was upset about hitting the deer, she just brushed it off, talking about how there are too many deer on the Cape anyway."

Winter thought for a moment before responding. "Well, I don't know her, so I cannot judge. But for me, killing a deer is not to be brushed off lightly. Deer are an integral part of

Wampanoag culture. Traditionally, when we kill a deer for food and clothing, we hold a ceremony to give thanks and to honor its life. Perhaps that was why you were attracted to my brother's deer. This is your way of honoring the deer you hit."

Jonathan considered this. "I do feel I owe the deer something, if that doesn't sound too crazy. It gave up its life in an accident that could have killed me, too. The wooden deer reminds me of how lucky I am and how precious life is." *Wow, where did that come from? Did I just use the word 'precious'?*

"That is a wonderful way to think about it. You were meant to have my brother's deer."

Winter and Jonathan kept talking, filling each other in on their backgrounds. Winter was half Native American, as her mother was Wampanoag. Her father, of Irish and British heritage with the last name of Jones, had left home when Winter was six and her brother Willy was eleven. The Jones family had a rough time, especially through the harsh Cape Cod winters, but they survived with the support of the tribal community in Mashpee. Winter, her mom, brother, and other family members were all skilled in making Native crafts and had built their own business, Wampanpoag Wares.

They discovered they were almost the same age. Winter was born less than two months before Jonathan, and they would both be twenty-one on their next birthdays. Winter was excited that it would be her *golden birthday,* as she would turn twenty-one on December 21st. Jonathan had never heard of this tradition and joked about how he had missed his golden birthday a long time ago, when he had turned eight in February of 1965.

The skyline of Boston rose before them, and Winter asked exactly where she should drop him off. Jonathan didn't want to tell her that he lived another twenty-five miles north of the city, so he told her to drop him off at North Station, and he would take the train the rest of the way.

"How far is the rest of the way?" Winter asked.

"Another twenty-five miles north," he said reluctantly.

"That's only another half hour and easier than driving in Boston. I'll just take you all the way."

Jonathan tried to talk her out of it, but she insisted. They talked nonstop for the rest of the trip.

During a pause in the conversation, Winter said, "Sorry the radio isn't working in this car. I see you have a guitar. What kind of music do you play?"

"Let me show you," Jonathan answered, reaching back to grab his guitar. "This is a song I wrote called 'When Will I Know?'" He strummed his guitar and sang.

"That was beautiful! It sounds a little bit like a Neil Young song I like."

"I like Neil Young, too. I like all kinds of rock, especially with a country, folk, or blues twist. The Grateful Dead is one of my favorite bands because they incorporate so many genres into their music. I jam with a few friends every week, and I've written almost enough songs for an album."

"Are you planning on a career in music? You said something about college earlier."

"I wanted to go to Newbury to study music, but my father insisted that I go to Bancroft and major in marketing so I can get a *real job*. He convinced me that if I had a degree in marketing, I could use it for anything, including the music business. He didn't mention how boring it would be. I feel like I'm wasting my time every moment I'm there."

"That seems like an awful way to live, being bored and feeling like you're wasting your time. Why don't you talk to your father? Tell him how you feel and that you want to make a change?"

"He's not easy to talk to. He pays my tuition and some of my other expenses. I would have to pay for music school on my own. Right now, I only have a part-time job at Shop 'n Save. And I still live at home."

"I didn't say it would be easy."

Jonathan turned away to look out the window. He had nothing to say to this last comment. It annoyed him that this girl he'd just met was giving him advice, but it annoyed him more that she was right.

Why can't I ever talk with Dad? Why can't he ever see that my interests aren't his interests?

He was so afraid of creating conflict in his family and more worried than he cared to admit about leaving home and making it on his own. He'd had too easy a life; it appeared that Winter had not.

As they neared his exit, Jonathan dropped their conversation to give her directions. It was just past noon when they pulled up in front of the large white Colonial with blue shutters and bright red door—patriotic colors, his dad always said. Winter pulled the VW bus into the driveway, passing the large rock with *The Family Rock* neatly painted on it in white.

"The Family Rock? That's funny," Winter said. The sound of her laughter drove away all of his doubts and worries.

"I know, but what's funnier is that I never told you my last name. It's Rock. My name is Jonathan Rock. I swear the main reason my dad bought this house was because of that rock. One of the first things he did was paint those words on it. He repaints it every year, so it always looks fresh."

"Well, that's the coolest name I ever heard, Jonathan Rock. It sounds like you were born to be a musician."

"Yeah, I've thought of that. Winter Jones is a pretty cool name, too." He shuffled to put his guitar back in its case. "Hey, do you want to come in and have lunch? You have a long trip back."

"No, that's alright. I'll stop at a rest area on the way back. It was a nice ride. Thanks."

"Thank YOU for bringing me all the way here. Can you get back to the highway from here okay?"

"Sure, no problem. And good luck with everything."

Jonathan couldn't think of anything else to say. He could have spent the rest of the day with her.

"Can I have your phone number in case I'm ever down your way again?" he asked.

"Sorry, we don't have a phone. But you know where to find me."

He put a ten-dollar bill on the seat for gas and got out of the bus.

"Thanks again, and goodbye, Winter Jones."

"Goodbye, Jonathan Rock."

He stood smiling and waving as the old, green-and-white VW Microbus headed back to the highway.

5

SATURDAY, JUNE 22, 2047

My grandfather pauses in his story, his eyes refocusing from the past to the present.

"Can I have some water?" he asks hoarsely.

"Of course, that was a lot of talking," I say, pouring him a glass of water from the pitcher on his bedside table. He picks it up with both hands and lifts it unsteadily to his lips.

"What a romantic story," I say warmly. "It makes me think about how Rafael and I met at a street fair in the North End, where he was working at a food stand. I ordered a salad, and he said he had just run out of lettuce but could give me a bowl of everything else. It was delicious. After we moved in together, *Everything Else Salad* became one of our favorite meals. Unfortunately, our story didn't end as successfully as yours and Grandma's."

"I know you told me you broke up. Remind me what happened."

I sigh heavily. "He came home one night toward the end of last summer and told me that an up-and-coming chef was opening a new restaurant in New York City, and he had offered Rafael a position as sous-chef. He accepted it without telling me anything about it. He'd been commuting to New York over the summer to attend a culinary institute, but had never said a word about relocating. It turns out he met a woman connected to this chef and was having an affair with her. The news hit me straight out of left field."

"You had no idea what was going on?"

"No! How could I with him in New York all week and me in Boston? We'd been together for over three years and talked about the future as if it would last forever. We had plans, and we'd support each other: I would write a book while working for the publishing company, and he would open his own restaurant.

I shrug. "I had no clue what was going on in New York. I guess I sound pretty naive." I stop talking and rub my eyes, trying to keep the tears at bay. Although it's been almost a year, it still hurts.

Grandpa watches me with a sorrowful look. He reaches out and takes my hand. "You are not naive, but you're very young. It may not help to hear that, but take it from this old man—you still have your whole life ahead of you. Live it and enjoy it the best you can."

I smile weakly and squeeze his hand. "Okay, enough about me. How did you ever meet up with Grandma again?"

Although the deep lines in his brow crease further as he concentrates, it's obvious that bringing the past to life again is a pleasure. "The insurance company did total my Mustang. I was so bummed about that. I loved that car. The money they gave me for it wasn't nearly enough to get a decent replacement. So, now I had no wheels, making it even more difficult to get back to the Cape. I hadn't told my parents about Winter or my unhappiness with college. I had no idea where to start, so, as usual, I said nothing and just continued working at the Shop 'n Save. I could walk there from my house."

"What happened with your old girlfriend, Michelle?"

"We officially broke up a week after the Fourth. We met at our favorite ice cream stand and had an unbelievably calm, mature conversation with no yelling, crying, or sarcastic comments. We hugged each other goodbye, and that was the end of that."

"Wow, that sounds almost too easy!"

"I thought so too, but I wasn't going to argue about it with Michelle," Grandpa says, chuckling at the memory.

"What was I saying before that?" he asks, a lost expression on his face.

"You were telling me how you met up with Grandma again," I remind him.

"That's right. Two weeks later, I asked my parents if I could borrow my mom's Woodie station wagon to visit a friend I had met on the Cape. I didn't mention that it was a girl, and they didn't ask. My father had been giving me a hard time about my car situation, but they were going away for the weekend and didn't need the station wagon, so I lucked out. I arranged to get a Saturday off from work and headed down to Cape Cod to find Winter."

6

SATURDAY, JULY 16, 1977

Jonathan opened the windows of the old Woodie to let in the Cape air. He rolled slowly over the Sagamore Bridge, thinking about the last time he crossed, heading home in the passenger seat of Winter's VW Bus. Thoughts of her played over and over in his mind, especially the last part of their conversation about how he was living his life. He had broken up with Michelle but had not made any other changes.

It was eleven when Jonathan took the exit towards Sandwich. He pulled into the grassy field next to the flea market, parked the station wagon, and walked over to the stalls. It was hard to believe it was only two weeks since he'd met Winter. Everything about the place was the same. The hot sun shone down on the same displays of crafts, old books, posters, paintings, jewelry, records, and general junk. This was promising because that meant Winter was most likely here again.

As he passed the lemonade stand, Jonathan saw the VW bus parked at the end of the row. He strolled toward the table that held the handmade crafts of which Winter and her family were so proud. No one was in sight. Jonathan paused momentarily, questioning his decision to show up without notice. But, he reminded himself, she had said, "You know where to find me." And there she was.

Winter appeared at the door of the bus and stepped down with an armful of items that she carried to the table. She was wearing short cut-off jeans and an oversized plain white tee shirt, tied up in a knot at her waist. A colorful beaded necklace hung around her neck, and several bracelets rattled lightly around her tanned arms. Her long dark hair was tied back in a ponytail. She was even more beautiful than he remembered.

Jonathan slowly approached as she finished arranging the items. Recognition dawned, and her face lit up into a broad smile, showing those crooked front teeth. Jonathan smiled back. Her reaction confirmed that he had made the right decision to come.

"Hello, Winter Jones."

"Hello, Jonathan Rock. I knew I'd see you again."

"Really? How did you know?"

"Maybe I trusted in the deer to bring you back."

Winter stepped from behind the table, opened her arms, and surprised him with a quick, gentle hug. Jonathan had just enough time to take in her scent, a combination of herbs, berries, and a hint of clean sweat. Although she had barely touched him, her calm, warm energy enveloped him. He felt removed from reality, as if he were in a movie instead of his boring life.

They slowly stepped back from one another.

"Excuse me, could you tell me how much this necklace is?" a voice asked from behind them.

Two women had walked over to the table. Winter turned her attention toward them to talk about the jewelry. She described the materials, the significance of the colors, and the amount of work that went into making them. Her explanation made the price she asked seem fair. The women haggled a bit, but Winter ended up selling them a necklace and two bracelets for twenty dollars.

"You're a good haggler," Jonathan said as the women walked away.

"Thanks, but I don't really like that part of this job. The money is good for things like food, gas, and paying the bills, but I prefer to talk about the items, the craft, and the symbolism, and teach people about Wampanoag culture."

Winter smiled as another customer came to the table. Jonathan sat on a folding chair, watching and listening as Winter went about her business. The crowd thinned as the sun got hotter and higher. Jonathan bought hotdogs, chips, and lemonade for lunch, and they talked as they ate.

"What have you been doing over the last two weeks?" Winter asked.

"Well, I officially broke up with Michelle."

"How did that go?"

"That was probably the best conversation we've ever had. Michelle was nice—not sarcastic at all. We agreed that breaking up was the right decision."

"I'm glad to hear that went well."

"Unfortunately, things didn't go well with my car. The insurance company totaled it, which bums me out. I loved that car."

"So, how did you get here?"

"I borrowed my mom's Woodie station wagon."

"That's fun! It could be friends with my VW bus."

Jonathan laughed at that thought. "I think they would make a great pair! What have you been up to?"

"This is our busiest time of year, so I've been delivering goods to stores up and down the Cape. In between, I help my mother and aunts sew, bead, weave, and make all our little touristy items."

"Do you ever have time to go to the beach?"

Winter laughed. "Not nearly enough, but that sounds like a great idea. It is too hot for anything else this afternoon, and it looks like most of the customers must already be there. Would you be able to go with me? Are you staying over tonight?"

"Yes, I don't have to be home until Monday afternoon. I'll sleep in the station wagon if I can find a place to park. It's plenty big enough. I've camped out in it before."

Jonathan helped Winter pack everything away on the bus. By the time the flea market ended at two, they were sweating and ready for the beach.

"So, where is this big station wagon of yours?" Winter asked.

"It's in the parking lot. You could drive me over there, and I'll follow you to the beach."

"Sure, but I have to take the bus back home and change. I know a place where you can park for the night. There's a general store down the street from my house. I know the people who run it. Let's stop there first so we can talk to them."

"That sounds great, thanks."

Now, the Woodie followed its friend, the Microbus, down unfamiliar back roads through the densely wooded town of Mashpee. After about twenty minutes, Winter pulled into the parking lot of The General Store. Winter introduced Jonathan to the Native American couple who ran the place, Noah and Molly. They agreed that he could park in the back. They'd keep the porta-potty unlocked for the night. Jonathan and Winter thanked them and bought snacks, drinks, and a bag of ice for the beach.

"They are so nice," Jonathan said as they left the store.

"Most people in Mashpee are. Many of us are part of the Wampanoag Tribe and consider ourselves family." She jumped into the Microbus. "Let's get to the beach. Wait here while I go home and change. My house is just down the street."

"But I could just follow you home and go from there."

"No, really, it's easier this way," Winter said. She took off before Jonathan could respond.

That's a little strange, Jonathan thought, as he filled his cooler with ice, beer, soft drinks, crackers, and cheese. He used the porta-potty to change into his bathing suit. He pulled a beer from the cooler and leaned against the car, sipping it while waiting for Winter.

"Hey, I'm back!"

Jonathan turned to see Winter standing beside the car.

"Where did you come from? It's like you just appeared out of thin air!"

Winter laughed, swinging a large, beaded cloth bag over her shoulder. She wore the oversized tee shirt as a short dress to cover her bathing suit.

"Just one of my Indian tricks. There's a path through the woods from my house."

They drove to the beach and claimed a spot near the grassy, rocky area away from the water, where it was less crowded. Winter unrolled a beautiful hand-woven blanket from her bag. They spread it out and weighed it down with the cooler, their bags, towels, and Jonathan's guitar case.

By then, it was after three-thirty. The sun still blazed in the sky, its intensity eased by a breeze off the ocean. Winter removed her tee shirt and ran to the water's edge. Her two-piece, flower-print bathing suit clung perfectly to her long, lean, tan torso. Jonathan followed and ran past her, making it a race. She laughed and ran to catch up. They both plunged into the cold ocean water, then emerged, sputtering and laughing. He took her into his arms for a wet, salty kiss. Winter threw her arms around his shoulders and returned the kiss. They parted, bobbing in the waves, as they held each other's gaze in silent communion.

Finally, they returned to their blanket, hand in hand, and broke out the cheese, crackers, and drinks. Jonathan had another beer, but Winter chose a Sprite. He strummed his guitar as they chatted about their interests. They laughed when they found out they were both in the middle of reading Stephen King's *The Shining*. Jonathan was enjoying it more than Winter—he was into scary stories and horror movies—while she preferred long family sagas and poetry. Jonathan admitted that he could never get into poetry, but they both loved books about travel.

Jonathan began to play the song "Ripple."

"I love that song," Winter said. "You say you are not into poetry, but you are into music. Songs are poems."

"You're right—songs are poems. I guess I need the music to appreciate the poem," Jonathan said and began to sing the words softly.

After five, most beachgoers packed up to head home for dinner. Jonathan and Winter had fallen into a peaceful silence, lying on the blanket. He put his arm lightly around her shoulders, and she turned toward him, placing her arm around his waist. Again, her touch felt light as a feather but full of calm energy. They lay comfortably in this way, Jonathan drowsing in the comfort of her aura. He gave a start when Winter sat up suddenly.

"We should get going," she said. "I didn't want to wake you, but it's almost six."

"Oh, sorry, I didn't know I was sleeping."

"You don't have to be sorry for sleeping."

Jonathan laughed, "I know, but still, I feel like I left you for a while, and I want to be with you as much as possible."

The words were out before he realized how serious they sounded. Winter looked at him for a long time. Then she said, "I want to be with you, too."

They embraced, this time more closely. Jonathan ran his hands down her long, thick ponytail, and they kissed softly before gazing deeply into each other's eyes.

Winter broke the silence. "This feels so good, so right. Sorry, I don't know how to say exactly what I mean."

"That's okay. I think this feels good and right, too," Jonathan said, embracing her again. They remained still for several more minutes.

"I should get you home, but I'd love to spend more time with you. Can you come out to dinner with me?" Jonathan asked.

"I can, but I need to change first. I just realized you don't have a place to shower or change your clothes." She peered at him for a moment. "I guess you could do that at my house," she said hesitantly.

"Sure, as long as it's okay with your mother."

"I told my mom a little about you. I'm sure it would be okay with her. It's just—" Winter hesitated and turned her eyes away.

"What is it? What's bothering you?"

"Okay. It's two things. First, you must understand that my family is pretty poor. We have food and everything else we need to survive, but not much more. Our house is very small—more like a cottage. It is clean but hasn't been painted or fixed up in years. My mom and I share one bedroom, and my brother has the other one. "

"Oh, Winter, I don't care about things like that. Look at me. I'm not exactly fancy with my Grateful Dead tee shirts and long hair, am I?"

"No, but you're pretty fancy with your big white house with the red door out in the suburbs."

"But that's not me. That's my parents. I can't stand it there."

"You say that, Jonathan, but I am afraid it is you, or at least part of you, as long as you live there. I am not saying that having a big house is bad. It's just that it is very different from what I have."

"And I'm trying to say that how much money you have or how big a house you have isn't important to me. I get what you're saying about coming from different backgrounds, though. So what's the other thing?"

"What other thing?"

"You said there were two things. The difference in the size of our houses is just one thing."

Winter hesitated again, collecting her thoughts before continuing. "The second thing is my brother, Willy. He is not easy to get to know. He can be unfriendly to the point of being mean if he doesn't like someone."

"And you think he won't like me for some reason?"

"You never know with him. Willy drinks and sometimes uses drugs, so you can't be sure how he'll react to anything or anybody. He is so different from how he was before he fought in Vietnam. He is filled with an anger that never completely goes away."

"How long was he there?"

"He was there for one year, which was long enough. He never talks about it, but we've all heard the horror stories."

Jonathan took Winter into his arms and caressed her head. "I'm sorry you have to deal with that. If you're uncomfortable with me going there, I can wash up with water I have in the car."

"Thank you, Jonathan. Let me talk to my mom about it and see how Willy is doing. Maybe you can meet them tomorrow."

"That sounds good. I'll drop you off at your house, and you can meet me at the store."

Winter gave directions to her house. She told him to stop a little before her driveway and let her out there. She gave him a quick hug and kiss, and they agreed to meet in half an hour.

Jonathan passed by slowly, taking in as much as he could of the house and yard. As she had said, it was small, set back from the road. Its white paint was peeling, and moss grew on the roof. A forest of thin, scrubby pine trees surrounded the yard. The VW bus was parked in the driveway behind a small, rusty old car with a flat tire. Piles of wood and carved figures surrounded a shed in the backyard. As Winter approached the steps to the front door, guarded by a large carving of a bear, a German shepherd bounded around the corner of the house, barking his greetings.

As he drove on, he thought about Winter's story, about her brother and mother, and what her life must be like. He thought about how lucky he had been in his life, at least from a financial point of view. Winter said her family had all they needed but not much more. How much more did his family have? A lot. He thought about all the furniture his mother constantly rearranged or replaced, the curtains, tablecloths, and decorations that changed with each season, the paintings from art galleries in Rockport, and the fine china and sterling silver reserved for special occasions. Not to mention the two vacations a year.

After parking the Woodie in back of the store, Jonathan washed up and used the porta-potty again to change. He decided to dress up, at least for him, and put on a pair of chino shorts and a dark green polo shirt. He switched from his flip-flops to leather sandals and did his best to brush out his hair and tie it neatly into a ponytail.

Satisfied with his appearance, he decided to have another beer from the cooler while waiting for Winter. *Waiting for Winter. That would be a good name for a song*, he thought, and began thinking of lyrics. Maybe he was a poet, after all.

"Hi, I'm back."

Jonathan jumped a little. Winter did tend to appear out of nowhere. She wore a beaded cotton dress and had draped her neck and arms with brilliant necklaces and bracelets.

"Hi, you look nice," he said as Winter got into the passenger side.

"Thanks. Could I have a sip of that?" she asked, noticing the beer can.

"Oh, this is almost done, and it's getting warm. I'll get you a new one," Jonathan said, reaching back to open the cooler.

"Okay, but I just want a little. I don't drink that much alcohol."

"That's okay. I'll drink the rest," he said as he opened the can and handed it to her.

Winter took a couple of long sips of the beer and handed the can to Jonathan.

"I wasn't sure if you drank, " Jonathan said.

"Not often, but I sometimes like a beer or glass of wine. I also like Margaritas, but only occasionally."

Jonathan laughed at that. "Margaritas? Have you heard that song 'Margaritaville' by Jimmy Buffet?"

"Yes, that is a fun song," Winter said, taking back the beer for another sip. "There's a Mexican restaurant not too far from here. Would you like to go there?"

"That would be great," Jonathan said, finishing the beer. "Just tell me how to get there. And, by the way, dinner is on me. I'm paying."

"Okay, thanks," Winter said without arguing.

La Cantina was an adobe-style building on the beach painted pink with strings of colored lights. Jonathan and Winter sat on the outside patio, sharing a massive order of nachos and a bowl of spicy chicken wings. They each had a large Margarita.

"That was delicious. Thank you," Winter said as they walked out to the beach after dinner.

"You're welcome," Jonathan said, taking her hand in his, "but I think we need some exercise after all that food.

"Definitely," she agreed. They left their sandals behind and ambled barefoot down the dark beach, lit only by lights reflecting on the water from nearby houses. The cool night air refreshed them after the heat of the day. As night fell, the sky became overcast, the stars just dim pinpoints. There was no moon.

"It's the new moon tonight," Winter said as they strolled hand in hand. "It is a time of new beginnings."

"That sounds good to me. I would like to begin again, with you," Jonathan said, taking her into his arms. He embraced her until a stray wave broke at their feet. They laughed and ran away from the water's edge.

They headed back to the car in silence, each unsure what to say and uncertain what a new beginning might mean. They had not discussed Jonathan's doubts about continuing in college or Winter's plans for the future. The silence continued as Jonathan drove back to Winter's house.

When they arrived at her house, Jonathan again parked on the road away from the driveway.

"This has been a great day," Winter said as she leaned over to give him a quick kiss. "Thank you, Jonathan.

Jonathan could not believe this had been just one day in his life. He felt like a completely different person from the one who woke up in his house that morning. He felt more like himself. He felt whole.

"Thank you, Winter. Can I see you again tomorrow? I don't have to go home until Monday."

"Of course, you can, but I have deliveries to make tomorrow. I have to go all the way out to Provincetown. Do you want to come and help me?"

"I would love to do that!" Jonathan said. "When will you leave?"

"Not too early. We usually sleep a little later on Sunday and make a big breakfast. Would you like to join us?"

"What about your brother?"

"Don't worry about him. I will not let him run my life."

"Okay, I guess I can come," Jonathan said hesitantly.

"I'll come by to get you around nine."

"See you then," Jonathan said, thinking that her idea of sleeping late was much different than his.

Winter reached over and kissed him again before getting out and heading to her house. He drove to the parking lot, arranged his sleeping bag and blankets in the back of the car, and thought about smoking some of the pot he had stashed in his duffel bag.

No, I don't need that, he thought, as memories of the day played in his head. He took the deer from his bag and placed it beside him.

"Thank you," he said, closing his eyes. Sleep came quickly and peacefully.

7
____

SUNDAY, JULY 17, 1977

T he birds woke Jonathan early, their happy songs entering through the partly open windows. He pulled on the chino shorts and polo shirt from last night that he had folded neatly the night before. His muscles felt stiff as he climbed out of the car and gulped in the fresh morning air. He stretched to get the kinks out, and thoughts of the previous day played in his mind. He felt good in both body and soul, better than he'd felt in a long time, his head clear of doubt and worry. *Be here now*, he reminded himself, on Cape Cod, on a beautiful summer day, waiting for the girl he loved to take him home for Sunday breakfast. *Yes, I love her*, he admitted to himself.

Jonathan sat on the tailgate of the station wagon and meditated in the quiet for several minutes. A pickup truck pulled into the parking lot. Noah exited the truck and started to unload it. Cases of soda, boxes of food and paper goods, and gallon jugs of water filled the back of the pickup.

Jonathan hopped off the tailgate and called out, "Good morning!"

"Good morning!" Noah called back. He was a tall, muscular

man with long black hair in a single thick braid that fell halfway down his back. "You're up early. Did you sleep well?"

"The birds woke me, but that's okay because I slept great. It was very quiet during the night. Let me help you carry some of that stuff."

"Thanks, I'd appreciate it."

They worked until everything was in the store. Jonathan helped stock the shelves, get the coffee brewing, and put out donuts, pastries, and muffins in anticipation of customers when the store opened at eight-thirty.

Once everything was set up and ready, Noah said, "You're a good worker, Jonathan. Thanks."

"No problem, I owe you for the parking spot," Jonathan replied. "I work at a Shop 'n Save back home, but we're closed on Sundays."

"We're allowed to open on Sundays because we serve food, like a restaurant. And we cater to tourists who want to buy souvenirs," Noah said, "mostly provided by your girlfriend." He winked.

Heat rose in Jonathan's face, and he realized he was blushing, although he wasn't sure why. It surprised him to hear the word *girlfriend* used to describe Winter, since they'd known each other for only a couple of days. He liked the sound of it, but something was missing. Michelle had been a girlfriend, but Winter was something much more.

"Sorry, I hope I got that right," Noah said, sensing Jonathan's discomfort. "It sure seemed like you two liked each other when you came in yesterday."

"Oh no, that's okay," Jonathan stammered. "I mean, yeah, we do like each other. I guess she is my girlfriend."

Noah burst out with a deep, booming laugh. "Oh, you make me jealous. What a joy to be young and in love! Of course, being old and in love is not too bad, either. My Molly is the only woman I ever wanted. I wish you and Winter the same luck we've had. You seem like a fine young man, and Winter is an exceptional young woman. She deserves to have a strong partner to help her through this life." He sobered. "Be kind to her."

"I will." Jonathan wondered how Noah assumed he would be with Winter *through this life*.

"Have you met Willy yet?" Noah asked, raising his eyebrows.

"No, not yet."

"Oh, man, you're in for a treat," Noah said.

"In what way?"

"You'll find out. Just take it easy around him."

"Okay, thanks for the advice," Jonathan said, smiling weakly.

Noah patted him on the back. "You're welcome. Like I said, just be kind."

The store door opened with a jangle of bells, and the first customer entered, looking for his Sunday morning coffee and doughnut. Noah waved Jonathan off with a smile and walked over to chat with the man. Jonathan went out to the parking lot to wait for Winter.

There she was, leaning against the station wagon, smiling her crooked-toothed smile. Her hair was loose today. She wore a short light cotton dress, decorated with patterns of colored beads.

"Good morning!" she called, walking toward him.

"Good morning!" he returned. He wrapped his arms around her for a soft kiss.

"Let's walk to my house," Winter said. She took his hand to show him a trail opening at the edge of the woods. "Here's my secret path.

"My mother is making enough pancakes to feed an army," she said as she led the way. "She cannot wait to meet you."

"You're making me nervous."

"Don't be nervous. She will love you."

"What about your brother?"

Winter hesitated for an instant. "I cannot make any promises about Willy, but if you just be yourself, he will see that you are a good person."

About five minutes later, the path ended on the margin of Winter's backyard. The German shepherd ran up to them, barking loudly with bared teeth. Jonathan shied away, but Winter patted the dog and calmed him.

"This is Max," she said. "He's friendly as long as he knows you belong here."

Jonathan hesitantly patted Max's back as they walked past the shed he had noticed the day before. Winter explained that this was Willy's workshop. They continued around the small house to the front door. They entered a living room with a couch and two mismatched chairs draped with woven blankets of bright colors. A large table strewn with paper, fabric, beads, paints, and basket-weaving materials took up most of the room. Watercolor paintings of the ocean, birds, flowers, and forest animals covered the walls. Jonathan noticed there was no TV.

The rich aromas of coffee brewing and bacon sizzling filled the house. In the compact kitchen to the left of the living room, Winter's mother shuffled between the stove, counter, and table. The table was set for four with plates and cups of different colors and patterns. Although mismatched, they went well together.

Jonathan could see the resemblance between the two women, although Winter's mother was heavier, had a darker complexion, and a more prominent nose. Her face burst into a happy grin upon seeing Winter and Jonathan.

"Good morning, welcome to our home," she called out, wiping her hands on a dishtowel.

"Good morning, Mrs. Jones. Thanks for inviting me," Jonathan said. He shook her outstretched hand.

"Please, call me Mary. I am so happy to meet you, Jonathan. Winter has told us many good things about you."

"Where's Willy?" asked Winter as her mom ran back to the kitchen to make sure the bacon didn't burn.

"He's taking a shower. He'll be out soon, then we can eat. Please sit. I hope it is not too hot in here."

"It's fine," said Jonathan. "It's nice out today, not as hot as yesterday. Everything smells delicious!"

Jonathan sat at the table while Winter helped her mother finish preparing breakfast. She served him coffee and orange juice and put a bowl of berries on the table. When the pancakes, piled high on a large platter, and bacon were ready, Mary called down the small hall at the back of the house, "Willy, breakfast is ready! Everyone is here!"

"Okay!" came a deep, muffled answer behind a door down the hall.

A moment later, Willy appeared, making the already small house seem even smaller. He was over six feet tall, and his plain white T-shirt stretched tightly over his chest and biceps. His long, black hair was bound, Native American-style, into two tight braids tucked behind his ears. His bronze face had the same prominent nose as his mother's.

Wow, this guy is a real Indian! Jonathan could not help thinking. He stood to meet Willy, wanting to be as polite and respectful as possible while showing a strong front.

"Hello, Willy, nice to meet you," Jonathan said, smiling slightly.

"Nice to meet you, too," Willy replied, grasping Jonathan's hand more firmly than necessary. He stared fiercely into Jonathan's eyes.

Jonathan returned the firm handshake and stared back, refusing to look away. Finally, Willy smiled and released his grip. His stare softened. He took in the platter of pancakes and bacon on the table. "Let's eat!"

They concentrated on the fluffy pancakes drizzled with real maple syrup, bacon from a local butcher, wild strawberries, and early blueberries. Jonathan was relieved not to have to make conversation while they ate. Eventually, the eating slowed down as their stomachs grew full.

"That was delicious, Mary," Jonathan said to break the silence. "Thank you."

"You are welcome. I am happy you enjoyed it."

Jonathan turned his attention toward Willy, still focused on his plate. He soaked up the last of his syrup with the final piece of pancake.

"I want to thank you, too, Willy."

"For what?"

"For carving the deer that I bought from Winter."

Willy looked up from his plate and gazed into Jonathan's eyes. His voice deepened as he said, "She told me about the deer you killed. That's too bad. I carved that deer after seeing a young buck standing at the edge of the woods in the backyard. It was twilight, and the sun lit up his antlers. It's sad to think of a beautiful creature like that losing his life for nothing."

"I agree," said Jonathan, a little shakily, surprised at the emotions that still rose when he thought about it. He chose his words carefully. "I felt terrible about it myself. The tow truck driver mentioned something about venison, so perhaps it was not a total waste of the deer's life. Also, your carving led me to Winter, which was a good thing."

"I hope so," Willy said, pushing away his empty plate.

"It was a very good thing," Winter said, giving Jonathan an encouraging smile.

"Winter tells me your last name is *Rock*," Mary said. "Where does that come from?"

"It was originally a French name, *Rocque*, anglicized at some point to *Rock*. My father's side of the family is all French Canadian. My mother's side is a mixture of Irish and British."

"Well, we share that side with you, anyway," Willy said. "That's where the name *Jones* comes from, at least from the British part. Our whole family got anglicized."

Mary rose from her chair and started clearing the plates.

"Willy, why don't you show Jonathan your workshop while Winter and I clean up?"

As they all stood, Winter shot a worried look toward her brother, who smiled and nodded at her as if to say, *It's okay.*

I hope so, thought Jonathan.

WILLY LED Jonathan down the short hallway that divided the back of the house in half, passing two closed bedroom doors and the bathroom. He led him out the back door to his workshop. Larger wooden sculptures in various states of completion surrounded the shed, and piles of uncut logs leaned against it. An earthy, wood smell welcomed them into the workshop. Metal tools hung on hooks along the walls, and pieces of wood, paints, varnishes, and brushes took up every inch of shelf space. A long workbench took up one entire wall. Photographs of deer, bears, raccoons, ducks, eagles, seagulls, and other creatures of the forest and sea covered the walls.

"What is this called?" Jonathan asked, picking up a small pointed tool from the workbench.

"Don't touch that," Willy said in a low, harsh voice. He grabbed it from Jonathan and replaced it. "Don't touch anything."

A tremor of fear ran down Jonathan's spine. "Okay, sorry," he said as calmly as possible,

Willy glared at him. "You're going to be even sorrier if you do anything to hurt my sister," he said. "You treat her right, or you have me to answer to. You understand?"

"Yes, I understand," Jonathan said. Anger mixed with his

fear. "I would never do anything to hurt Winter. You don't need to threaten me."

Willy stepped closer and looked him in the eye. "It's not a threat."

Jonathan held his gaze, which wasn't easy.

"Want to see what I'm talking about?" Willy said, raising his voice. He shoved Jonathan in the chest with two rigid fingers.

Jonathan's body tensed, ready to fight, although butterflies fluttered in his stomach.

"Hey, what's going on?" called Winter. She came to the door of the work shed and peered in at the two men frozen in place.

"Nothing. Just having a little chat with your boyfriend," Willy said, giving Jonathan a warning look.

Jonathan relaxed. "Yeah, everything's cool. We're just talking."

Winter eyed them skeptically. "We should leave for Provincetown soon, Jonathan. Let's start loading the bus."

THE WARM WIND through the open window blew Winter's hair back in dark waves as she drove along Route 6 through the middle of the Cape. Jonathan had grabbed his guitar from the station wagon before they hit the road. On impulse, he took the deer along for the ride, too. Now, with the deer standing on the dashboard as his audience, Jonathan strummed his guitar, working a few chords repeatedly in different combinations.

"What was going on with Willy back there? I hope he wasn't giving you a hard time."

"Don't worry about it. Let's not talk about Willy. It's too beautiful a day." He picked out measures of a new tune. "Tell me what you think about these songs I'm working on."

Jonathan played and sang while Winter drove and listened, smiling with encouragement. He alternated soft folk rock with more fast-paced tunes. His voice was not perfect, but his guitar playing was well-executed and sounded professional.

"I love your music, and I can tell you love making it. Have you thought of cutting your own record?"

"I have almost enough songs for an album, but it's a lot of work. And it's expensive to rent a recording studio. I'll need a good singer and other musicians to make it a reality. The guys I play with aren't enthusiastic about anything but jamming."

When they arrived in the crowded little town that marked the end of Cape Cod, it took all of Winter's attention to navigate through the narrow streets packed with both foot and vehicle traffic. The ocean of tourists parted slowly for them as the bus eased past small shops full of silver jewelry, tie-dyed shirts, leather sandals, records, books, and souvenirs. Art studios and restaurants with outdoor tables added to the congestion of the main street. A large white church loomed on a hill, and the tall, square tower of the Pilgrim monument stood guard over the town.

Jonathan jumped out of the bus and directed Winter as she backed into a small space in front of the tourist shop. He helped her unload the Wampanoag Wares items. The shop owner rewarded them with a check for the last two weeks' sales. It was sizable as they had entered the Cape's busiest tourist season.

"This calls for a celebration," Winter said as they walked down Commercial Street, window shopping in the eclectic mix of shops. The scent of patchouli emanated from several. They stopped at a seafood restaurant for lunch and sat on its outside deck. It overlooked the harbor, with its long pier stretching out past a narrow beach that divided the backs of the houses and shops from the waterline. Colorful fishing boats, sailboats, and motorboats crowded the docks or slipped quietly through the harbor. A diverse group of people walked along the pier and the beach: families with dogs, long-haired hippies, elderly folks with canes, and couples of every age, race, and gender combination imaginable.

"Can I get you something to drink?" asked the waiter.

"I'll have a Miller Lite," Winter said, surprising Jonathan.

"I'll have one of those too."

"Okay, but can I see some ID?" the young waiter asked.

Jonathan and Winter held their driver's licenses up for inspection.

"Thanks," the waiter said. "I love that the drinking age here is eighteen. I come from Pennsylvania, where it's twenty-one."

They ordered fried clams, french fries, and a lobster roll. They shared the order as they watched the harbor scene. Jonathan liked that he didn't constantly have to make conversation with Winter. They were both comfortable with companionable silence.

After lunch, they went to the beach and sat in the sand with their backs against a large rock. Jonathan put his arm around Winter, and she laid her head on his shoulder. They immersed themselves in the sounds of seagulls crying, boat horns deeply booming, and people chattering around them. The warm, briny air made them feel sleepy.

"Provincetown is fun to visit, but I wouldn't want to live here," Winter said. "But I'd love it if we had our own shop, where we could sell our crafts. I wouldn't have to run all over the Cape delivering our stuff to other vendors. I would have a corner for customers to buy coffee and homemade baked goods, with a few chairs and tables to sit and relax. Maybe I would have a shelf of books about Cape Cod and Native culture."

"That would be great! I've always wanted to have my own jam space, where musicians could play together and perform for small audiences. And, yeah, sell drinks and snacks and maybe records on the side."

"And you could sell some of my things on the side, too," Winter added playfully.

"And I could play my guitar on weekends for background music in your shop."

They hesitated and looked at each other. Then, at the same time, they said, "We could do it all in one place!"

They laughed and hugged each other, then grew quiet. Winter reached up and ran her hand over Jonathan's unshaven face, and he bent down to kiss her. Thoughts of all the hurdles they would have to climb over for their idea to become a reality invaded their minds.

"That sounds like a great idea, but I'm not sure how it could happen," Winter said. She ran her hands down the length of his arms. "Especially since you don't live on the Cape."

Jonathan sighed deeply before responding. "No, I'm not sure how it would work, either. But I'd like to explore the idea. I feel so much freer here, and you know I'm not happy with my life back home. This could be the escape, or direction, I'm looking for."

"I would love for you to live on the Cape, but that would not be easy for you. Also, it may seem like a good idea now, but have you ever been here in the winter?"

"No, but I know a girl named Winter who could help me through it." He smiled with his tease.

"I'm not sure how that would work," Winter said, pulling away.

He sat up. "I'm sorry. Maybe that wasn't the right thing to say. We've only known each other for a few days. But I feel like I've always known you, like I was just waiting to meet you."

"I feel the same," she agreed, "but as you say, it has been a short time, and many things are uncertain right now."

She laid her head back on his shoulder. "I'm tired. I need to close my eyes for a few minutes."

"Okay, me too. Then we'll head back. I'll drive."

AFTER MAKING deliveries to two more stores and taking the scenic ride down the coast, they arrived back in Mashpee at six, tired and hungry. There was no sign of Willy, Mary, or Max, so Jonathan took a quick shower while Winter looked for something for supper.

"Let's grill a couple of hamburgers and eat outside on the picnic table," she said, loading a tray with the essential items.

"Sounds good."

As they sat at the picnic table waiting for the burgers to cook, they heard a car pull up in front of the house. After the sounds of hollered goodbyes, Mary, Willy, and Max came around the house into the backyard. Willy carried a large cooler, which he set on the ground near the picnic table.

"Hello!" Mary called. "We just got back from Aunt Elizabeth's. We had dinner there. How was your day?"

"Everything went fine," Winter said. She glanced at Willy, who pulled a beer from the cooler. "Jonathan was a big help."

"That's good to hear. Have a beer," Willy said. "Hey, that rhymes! I'm a poet, and I don't know it." He handed the beer to Jonathan.

"Thanks," Jonathan said. He wondered how many beers Willy had drunk already.

"I'm glad to hear your day went well. Time for me to head in. Have a good night," Mary said.

"Good night!" they all said at once.

Winter took the hamburgers off the grill, and she and Jonathan made up their plates. Willy left them alone to eat. He threw a ball for Max and drank his beer. When the sun sank behind the trees, Willy put a stop to the game of fetch and produced a couple of lanterns from the shed, which he set on the table. He took two more beers out of the cooler, handed one to Jonathan, and sat down with them.

"So, you two had a good day today?" he asked, taking a big gulp.

"Yes, we did," Winter replied. "We delivered to Province-town, Orleans, and Yarmouth. Each one had a good check for us."

"Good to hear." Willy pointed to Jonathan's guitar leaning against the picnic table. "Do you play that thing?"

Jonathan picked up the guitar, slung the strap over his shoulder, and played a sequence of riffs, embellishing them with overly dramatic finger work.

"Okay, looks like you can play a little. Hey, I didn't finish showing you my workshop. Want to take a look now?"

Jonathan hesitated, but Winter said, "Go ahead, you guys do that, and I'll clean up here."

Jonathan followed Willy into the shed with its lingering aroma of raw wood. He was once more impressed by the sheer number of tools and materials in the small building. Willy picked up the tool Jonathan had asked him about during their earlier encounter.

"This is an awl. I use it to make holes and to draw fine lines in the wood."

Willy explained how he made his carvings. First, he chose a log or piece of wood and studied it until the essence of the animal within became apparent to him. He showed Jonathan the different carving tools and demonstrated how each was used as he worked on a raccoon carving.

He handed Jonathan a small rectangular piece of wood and asked, "What animal do you see in this?"

Jonathan studied it. "I see a fish, probably a cod."

Willy laughed and handed him a small, sharp pocketknife. "Okay, now all you have to do is find your codfish in the wood. You can keep this knife until you've finished."

"Thank you for showing me all this," Jonathan said. "Your work is excellent. Where did you learn how to carve like that?"

"My Uncle Samuel was a master woodcarver. When I was little, I could sit and watch him for hours. As soon as I was old enough to hold a knife, he taught me everything he knew. He died of cancer a few years back, but left me all his tools."

"Sorry about your uncle."

"Yeah, life's a bitch. Hey, want a little nightcap?"

Willy reached under the workbench and pulled out a bottle of Jim Beam and two small paper cups.

"Sure," Jonathan said. Willy's presence was still intimidating, and Jonathan felt a little nervous about how to respond to him. Obviously, alcohol played a big part in Willy's mood change, now friendly, but Jonathan knew from experience that it could quickly turn things in the other direction.

He took the cup Willy offered and sipped the golden-brown liquid. He stifled a shudder as it burned through his throat into his stomach. He wasn't used to drinking straight alcohol. Willy tipped his cup back, drained it in one large gulp, and pulled two wooden stools up to the workbench. Settling down on one of the stools, Willy poured another cupful, took a sip, and pointed to the other stool.

"Come join me."

Jonathan took another sip from his cup and hesitantly sat on the stool.

"What are you guys up to in here?" Winter asked, appearing at the door. "It looks like you have your own little bar going here."

"Just having a little after-dinner drink. Is that a problem?" Willie asked, a bit of a challenge in his voice.

"No, that's okay, but I was wondering if Jonathan could help me load some boxes on the bus so I am ready for tomorrow."

"I'd be happy to help," Jonathan said eagerly. "Bye, Willy, thanks for the drink." He picked up his cup and drained it.

"You're welcome," Willy said as he swallowed the rest of his second drink.

"Don't stay out here too long, Willy. It's getting late," Winter said as she and Jonathan headed out the door.

Willy picked up the bottle and poured another shot.

"I DON'T REALLY HAVE any boxes ready for tomorrow. I just wanted to save you from Willy," Winter said once they were out of earshot of the shed.

"Thanks, I needed that," Jonathan said, laughing.

He put his arms around her. She returned his embrace and leaned back against the bus as he moved closer to kiss her.

"You taste like whiskey."

"Is that a bad thing?"

"Not too bad," she said as they kissed again.

"Hey, you should probably head back to your car," Winter said, pulling away. "I'll walk you over there."

"Okay," Jonathan said. "Can I use your bathroom first?"

Winter laughed. "Of course you can. Just be quiet. My mom is probably asleep already."

Instead of taking the path through the woods, they strolled down the dark street, lit only by the lights of the houses they passed. Many people still sat outside, talking and laughing in the mild evening. Small fires burned in pits in a few yards, where children and dogs ran and played around them. Winter called out "Hello" to all her neighbors, and they responded in kind. A few groups invited Winter to join them, but she politely declined.

"People are so friendly around here, and they're all outside," Jonathan said, holding Winter's hand as they walked along. "We hardly know anyone in our neighborhood, and you only occasionally see them outside."

"That's because the people in your neighborhood are all inside their big, air-conditioned houses, watching TV. These houses aren't air-conditioned, and some don't have TVs. We rely on each other for entertainment. We talk, tell stories, sing songs, eat, drink, and play games together."

They walked hand in hand in silence, and soon they were at The General Store, where the station wagon was parked. Woods surrounded them on both sides of the street, and it was very dark, the store lights guiding them toward the hulking big box of the car. It seemed like days since he last saw the Woodie, but it had only been since morning. So much had happened in a single day.

Jonathan unlocked the car and opened all the doors and windows to let in cooler air. He opened the tailgate and sat on it with Winter. She sighed deeply, and Jonathan put his arm around her shoulders.

"Are you okay? What are you thinking about?" Jonathan asked, rubbing circles on her back.

She remained quiet, then said, "I am tired of thinking."

"I'm sorry," Jonathan said, continuing to massage her back. "Do you want to go home? I can give you a ride."

"There is nothing for you to be sorry about, and no, I don't want to go home," she said. "That feels good."

She turned to him, and they put their arms around each other. Their lips met in a deep kiss. Jonathan slid his hands down the length of her cotton dress. Winter rubbed one hand down his side, the other caressing the back of his neck. Slowly, as their hands continued to search each other's bodies, they lay down in the back of the station wagon.

Jonathan's hand strayed under Winter's dress, up her leg, over her hip, and rested on her breast. Winter slid her hand under his shirt and ran it over his chest.

She pulled back when he slid his hand down her belly to her panties.

"Sorry, I didn't mean to do that," she said. "I'm just a bit nervous."

"It's okay. I don't want to rush you into anything. We can stop if you're not comfortable."

"It's just that, believe it or not, I've never done this before. I've gone out on dates with a few guys but never got to this point with anyone. I was waiting until I met the right person."

"I understand. What do I have to do to be the right person?"

"Just be yourself, Jonathan Rock," Winter said. She pulled him close once again. "Just be gentle."

Her response surprised him. "Are you sure? It's okay if you want to wait."

"I've waited long enough," Winter said. "Oh, and do you have protection?"

"I do."

She pulled her dress over her head and cuddled into the sleeping bag.

Jonathan got out, closed the tailgate, and got back in by the driver's side door. He closed the windows partway, locked the doors, and climbed into the back to join her.

He was gentle. Winter was glad she had waited.

8

MONDAY, JULY 18, 1977

The station wagon shook under the pounding of fists along its side and back.

"Hey! Wake up in there!"

"It's Willy!" Winter cried. She quickly pulled on her clothes under the sheet they had thrown over them.

Jonathan pulled on his shorts and tee shirt. "Stop hitting my car!" he yelled. "You're going to break a window!"

"You come out of there, you creep! And Winter, you come out too!"

Jonathan and Winter climbed into the front seat. He fumbled for the car keys. The dark orange glow of near-dawn hung over the parking lot.

"Maybe we should just take off on him," Jonathan said as Willy beat on the driver's side door.

Willy put his fingers through the two inches of open space at the top of the window and pulled hard on it. "If you don't come out, I'll rip this window out!"

"Stop it, Willy!" Winter said firmly. "Calm down! Just let us come out, and we'll talk. You're scaring us. Back away so we can get out."

Willy let go of the window and backed up a few steps, his eyes wild. Jonathan opened the door and got out on the driver's side while Winter exited the passenger side. Willy lunged at Jonathan and shoved him into the side of the car. Fumes of stale sweat, beer, and whiskey drifted around him.

"Now, get out of here, rich white boy. You think you can just come down here, sing some songs, and fuck my sister in the back of your car like she's trash."

Jonathan reached into the pocket of his shorts and grasped the pocket knife Willy had given him last night. He debated whether or not to take the knife out. Could he use it if he had to?

Winter dashed around the car and started to pound on Willy with both fists. "It's not like that! You're still drunk. You don't know what you're talking about. Leave us alone!"

Willy took Winter's hands to still them and glared into her eyes. "You're the one who doesn't know what's going on here." His voice was loud and agitated. "I'm just trying to protect you."

Jonathan left the knife in his pocket and stepped towards them. "You don't need to protect her from me. I told you yesterday I'd never hurt her."

"And I told you to get out of here. NOW!" He leaped toward Jonathan again, but Winter locked both arms around his waist, holding him back with difficulty.

"It's okay, Jonathan," she pleaded. "Please just go. I can take care of this. He'll calm down once you leave."

"It's not okay," Jonathan replied, his anger and worry for Winter overcoming his fear. "I won't leave you with him like this."

"I've seen him like this before. He won't hurt me. Just go. I'm sorry. Please go!"

Winter was losing the fight to keep Willy from charging. Jonathan jumped in the car, started it up, and put his foot on the gas just as Willy broke free from Winter's grip. He drove forward several feet, opened the window, and yelled, "I love you!" in Winter's direction. The Woodie screeched out of the parking lot.

"WHAT IS THE MATTER WITH YOU?" Winter shouted.

Willy's eyes glazed over as he stared at her. "I need to protect you."

"No, you don't. You need to take care of yourself. You are a mess!"

Winter turned and ran toward the wooded path to the house. Willy followed slowly. As the sun rose, the sky above them glowed a brighter orange. When Winter realized Willy was far behind, she slowed to a walk. She breathed deeply and focused on the path ahead, trying to rid her mind of the images of Willy's attack.

What is Jonathan thinking right now? Would he ever come back?

She pushed those thoughts to the back of her mind. Suddenly, she sensed movement. A large, dark shape slipped across the path where it opened into the yard—a deer. It stopped and looked at her with its head raised, showing off its three-pointed antlers. Its soulful eyes stared into hers as if trying to communicate with her. She held its gaze, holding her body as still as the buck's. The sound of footsteps on the path alerted the deer. It dropped its eyes from Winter's and disappeared without a sound into the shadowed woods.

Winter crossed the yard quickly to the back door. She had no desire to see or talk to Willy. He would probably crash on the cot he kept in the shed and sleep off his hangover. Not wanting to wake her mother, she tiptoed down the hall past the bedrooms and lay on the living room couch to rest her eyes and soothe her mind for a few minutes.

She didn't expect to fall asleep after Willy's aggressive

attack, so she was surprised when her mother's soft call woke her.

"Winter? Are you okay?"

Winter sat up. She looked around the room and at her mother before remembering why she was in the living room, not in her bed. The events of the early morning streamed back into her conscience. She put her head into her hands and sobbed.

Mary took her daughter in her arms and rocked her. She rubbed Winter's back and murmured words of comfort. Finally, Winter's sobbing subsided, and she looked up at her mother. Her eyes felt swollen from crying.

"I know you didn't sleep in your bed last night. You were with Jonathan?" Mary asked. "You are a grown woman, and I trust your judgment, but something is wrong. Is there anything I can do?"

"You can kick my brother out of this house."

Mary sat back from Winter and studied her doubtfully. "What do you mean? What does Willy have to do with this?"

"He has everything to do with it. Jonathan and I were in his car over at The General Store, and—and we fell asleep. Willy woke us up, pounding on the car and yelling at us. He attacked Jonathan and pushed him against the car. He scared us to death. He threatened Jonathan and made him leave. If I hadn't grabbed Willy around the waist and held him back, I think he would have beaten him up."

Winter's eyes filled again as she told her story. "After this, I don't know if Jonathan will ever come back."

Mary smoothed her daughter's hair with her fingers as she processed the scene Winter had painted for her.

"I am so sorry. There is no excuse for this. I will have a serious talk with Willy and see that he apologizes to you and Jonathan."

"More than an apology is needed. He was still drunk at five

o'clock in the morning. He could have hurt Jonathan badly. Or me. We can't keep allowing things like this to happen. He already got a warning from the police after that bar fight back in March. And how is he supposed to apologize to Jonathan now? He chased him right off the Cape. I can't even call him because we don't have a telephone in this house."

Mary stood and gazed silently out the front window for a few moments. "You need to take a long shower and calm yourself down," she said. "We'll talk later." She headed for the kitchen to make breakfast.

Winter took a few deep breaths and headed to the bathroom. She would follow her mother's advice about taking a shower, but she didn't believe talking would solve this problem. She needed to take action. As the water pounded on her head and ran down her body, cleansing away the bad memories of the morning, one image remained: the deer calmly looking into her eyes. She knew what she had to do.

After drying off, she dressed in light cotton pants and a beaded blouse. She worked her hair into two long braids and thought more about the present state of her life. Spending the last two days with Jonathan and talking about his inner conflicts made her think about where she was heading.

Overall, she was content. She loved working with her mother and the community of Mashpee. She loved Cape Cod and didn't want to live anywhere else. But with Willy's behavior, this house was becoming too small for them all. She loved her brother deeply, but things couldn't continue the way they had for too long.

The aroma of fresh-baked blueberry muffins wafted down the hall as Winter drifted toward the kitchen, still searching for the right words to express her thoughts and feelings to her mother. Mary sat at the kitchen table, grasping a large coffee mug in both hands. She stared into the depths of the brown liquid as if seeking answers to her problems. When she glanced up at her daughter, Winter noticed her eyes looked red and watery, as if she had been crying.

"Oh, Momma," Winter said softly. She bent down to hug her. The words *I'm sorry* threatened to escape her lips before Winter caught herself. She was not going to apologize when she had done nothing wrong. She needed to be firm in her decision and find a way to make her mother understand.

Mary returned the hug and gently pushed her away. "Have a muffin. They just came out of the oven."

Winter poured herself coffee, put a muffin on a plate, and sat at the table beside her mother. Conflict between these two women was rare, which made this situation more complicated. Neither spoke as they ate their breakfasts. Winter braced herself to tell her mother her plans.

"I have to see Jonathan to talk to him. I need to go to his house."

Mary hesitated before responding. "That is not a good idea for many reasons. Why don't you just call him first? You could use the payphone at The General Store. Or Auntie Anne would let you use hers."

"No, I cannot just call him. I have no idea what he is thinking right now. I need to see him in person. If I leave by nine-thirty, I can get to his house by noon, before he has to go to work. I need to make sure things are okay between us and make plans to see him again. I'd be home by dinnertime."

"What will I do if I need the Microbus? It is not just your car. Besides, it is old and needs new tires. That is a long trip for it to make for the second time this month. I could also use your help to make some pieces today. This is our busiest time of the year. Aunt Elizabeth and Linda will be here soon to work with us."

"The bus will be okay, and I can run out and get you anything you need before I go." She looked firmly into Momma's eyes. "I have to do this."

"I am sorry, Winter, but I cannot allow this. It is too rash a decision. Jonathan may still be too upset to talk, and it could make matters worse to show up today, before he can see things more rationally. Let things calm down, call him later today or tomorrow, and make plans to meet again. In the meantime, I will talk to Willy and make sure he understands that he is to treat you and Jonathan with respect."

Before she could respond, Winter was interrupted by the sound of the back door banging open. Footsteps staggered down the hall. Willy appeared at the kitchen doorway, a sorrowful look in his bleary eyes.

"I'm sorry. I guess I got a little carried away last night," he mumbled.

"A *little* carried away? Is that what you call it?" Winter said, facing him with carefully controlled fury. "You attacked Jonathan and me like a wild animal. You made me ashamed of this family."

"Stop right there, Winter," Mary said. She rose swiftly from the table and stepped between them. "That's enough!"

"I'm the one who's had enough," Winter countered. "I need to go to Jonathan."

Willy shuffled to the table, sat down heavily, and put his head in his hands. Mary turned to Winter. "Okay, go. Go to Jonathan. I will straighten this out with Willy. But we will all have to talk about this together soon. That includes Jonathan if he chooses to be part of this family."

At this last statement, both Willy and Winter stared at their mother in astonishment.

JONATHAN SLOWED down a couple hundred yards from The General Store. He looked in the rearview mirror. But Willy and Winter were not in sight. *Should I go back, or would that cause*

more trouble? There was no reasoning with Willy in his current state, and Winter had been adamant about Jonathan leaving. She seemed sure her brother wouldn't hurt her. Jonathan sure hoped so. He put his foot on the gas. Waves of doubt, worry, and anger crashed through his mind.

Movement in the trees at the side of the road caught his attention. He slowed to a stop, remembering the encounter with the deer. There was nothing but the forest, lit by the orange-pink hue of sunrise. Why did he feel like he was being watched?

I've got to go. He stepped again on the accelerator and headed for home. But he felt more like he was leaving home behind.

Over two hours later, he took the exit toward his house and glanced at the clock. It was eight-thirty. He had hoped to get home after his father left for work, but the early morning traffic, before the rush hour built up, had been light. Stopping for coffee had not taken up enough time. Despite the caffeine, he was so tired now he feared his eyes would close if he drove any longer. He pulled to the side of the road in front of his house. His father's car was still in the driveway. *Damn!*

He parked and got out, then opened the tailgate and surveyed the jumble of sheets, blankets, and towels covering the tangled sleeping bag. Pulling back a blanket, he found the wooden deer. He picked it up and rubbed its back. Looking into its black shining eyes, he said, "What am I going to do? Please help me."

"Hey! You're home early!"

Jonathan turned to see his father, briefcase in hand, gray suit jacket slung over his arm, white shirt buttoned down, blue-striped tie tightened, ready to crunch numbers in his office all day.

"Yeah, I got an early start to avoid rush hour traffic and have some time to relax and clean up before work." Jonathan put the deer back under a blanket. He hadn't shown the deer to his parents after the Fourth of July weekend, when he wasn't sure if he'd see Winter again. After this morning's events, he was sure about Winter, but not of his next move.

"What's this? How did this happen?" his father asked. He set his briefcase on the ground and ran his hand over a crack in the woodgrain on the side of the Woodie. Jonathan looked at the damage and envisioned Willy kicking and punching it.

"Oh wow! I didn't notice that. Someone must have backed into me in a parking lot or something."

"Really? And where exactly were you?" his father asked, looking into the back of the station wagon. "I thought you were staying with a friend. It looks to me like you were sleeping in the car."

"My friend's house had no room, so I slept in the station wagon. I've done that before when I camped at those music festivals."

"I know, but this hippie stuff has got to stop! First, you wreck your car, and now you damage your mother's. And who is this friend, anyway?"

Okay, time to start laying it on the line. Jonathan kept telling himself he needed to get out from under his parents' shadow and live his own life. That wouldn't happen unless he spoke up, expressed his feelings, and told them his plans. Even though his plans were not solid, with countless issues to resolve along the way, he was sure of one thing: His plans would involve Winter. That meant quitting school and moving to the Cape.

Jonathan closed the tailgate of the station wagon and took a deep breath as he turned to face his father. "First of all, I didn't wreck my car. I hit a deer in the road that I couldn't avoid. Second, I did not damage Mom's car. Someone else did that, and I just noticed it now. And third, the friend I was visiting was a girl I met on the weekend of the Fourth. She lives on the

Cape, and I—I have very strong feelings for her and want to continue seeing her."

"I see," said his father, impatiently. He looked at his watch and picked up his briefcase. "It looks like we have a lot to talk about, but I have to get to work. I'll come back at lunchtime, and we'll talk then."

WINTER TOOK the exit off Route 128, remembering it from driving Jonathan home only two weeks ago. She had made good time, and it was a little before noon as she pulled up in front of *The Family Rock*. She parked the Microbus on the street in front of the house, looked at the rock, and smiled for the first time that day. She was happy to see the station wagon parked in the driveway. Jonathan was home. She stepped along the walkway toward the bright red front door. *I hope Jonathan answers, not one of his parents.*

The doorbell chimed inside the house, surprising Jonathan. "I'll get it," he said to his mother, who was making sandwiches for lunch in the kitchen.

He opened the door and stepped back at the sight of Winter standing on his doorstep. A nervous smile played around her lips, her dark-brown eyes flitting from him to the inside of the house. "Is this the house of the Family Rock?" she asked playfully.

"Oh my god, Winter! What are you doing here?" Jonathan stepped out and gave her a tremendous bear hug. They clung to each other briefly before Jonathan held her at arm's length. He looked deeply into her eyes, which brimmed with tears.

"I had to come see you to make sure you were alright. That *we* were alright."

"We are alright, Winter, but I'm not sure about everyone else. That will be the hard part." He hesitated. "My dad will be home soon. He wants to *have a talk.* You probably don't want to be here for that. Maybe you should take a ride and come back a little later so I can introduce you."

Jonathan's father's car rolled into the driveway.

"Too late," Winter observed. She grasped Jonathan's hand firmly. "I would like to be with you for this."

"Okay, but don't tell me I didn't warn you," Jonathan said, squeezing her hand in return.

As Mr. Rock walked to the door, he raised his eyebrows at the VW Microbus parked on the street and the young woman holding his son's hand on the doorstep.

"Hi, Dad, this is Winter, the girl from Cape Cod I told you about."

"Hello, Mr. Rock. It's nice to meet you," Winter said, extending her hand.

"Hello," Mr. Rock replied. He shook her hand hesitantly. "Winter? That's an unusual name."

"Not if you were born on December 21st!" Winter said with a playful tone.

Jonathan laughed, but his dad remained serious.

"I see," Mr. Rock said, "Let's go inside before all the cool air gets out." They entered, and Mr. Rock firmly closed the front door.

Winter shivered as she walked into the house, where two air conditioning units did their job. Before her, a curving staircase ran up to the second floor. She surveyed the large rooms on each side of the front entrance hall—a formal dining room to the left, and a living room to the right, both furnished impeccably. *Everything matches,* she thought. Oil paintings of still lifes, landscapes, and city scenes decorated the walls.

"Hello!" Mrs. Rock called out. She appeared in the hallway toward the back of the house and stopped, surprised, at the sight of Winter. She gave Winter an uncertain smile.

Winter smiled back at the pretty, red-haired woman. *So that's where Jonathan gets the red in his hair.*

"Mom, this is Winter. She's the girl I told you about." Jonathan had filled his mother in about Winter. In typical fashion, his mom said something like, "Oh, that's nice," which had ended the conversation.

"Hello, Winter," his mom said, shaking hands. "What an unusual name!"

"Apparently not if you're born on December 21st," Mr. Rock answered in a slightly sarcastic tone. "Let's sit down." He led them into the kitchen.

Winter tried not to look too amazed at the vast kitchen, which took up the whole back of the house. It had not one but two ovens, endless counter and cabinet space, and a polished, wood-topped island in the middle. A long table ran along the back wall, in front of a large window overlooking a backyard with an in-ground pool. A door off the kitchen led to a large wooden deck.

As they walked toward the table, Mr. Rock pulled Jonathan back from the women and spoke quietly, "Winter shouldn't be here for this conversation. We've only just met her. Why don't you ask her to wait outside in that hippie van of hers? She can come in for lunch afterward."

Jonathan shook his father's hand off his arm. "No, I want her to be here. She is too important a part of this."

Mr. Rock sighed and headed for the table, shaking his head.

"Should I put the food out now?" Mrs Rock asked.

"No, we need to talk first," Mr. Rock said brusquely, and they took their places.

"So, Winter," Mr Rock began, "What brings you here to visit? Jonathan was just there on the Cape this morning."

"He left before I could say goodbye. He invited me to come up here to visit sometime. I had a free day today, so here I am!"

Jonathan added, "I'll call Mark and ask him to take my shift today. I want to show Winter around."

Mr. and Mrs. Rock exchanged a puzzled look. "Will Winter be staying overnight? Will she sleep in her vehicle?" Mr. Rock asked.

"Oh no, I will drive back tonight. I have to get back to work tomorrow," Winter said.

"Where do you work?" Mrs Rock asked.

"My mom, brother, and I own a business with my aunts and a cousin. We make hand-made Native American crafts and supply them to several stores on the Cape. Summer is our busy season."

"The name of their company is Wampanoag Wares." Jonathan said. "Winter's mother is almost full-blood Wampanoag."

"You must be proud of that heritage," Mrs. Rock said. "I have always admired Native American culture."

Winter smiled. "Thank you. I am very proud of it."

"And what about your father?" Mr. Rock asked. "Is he part of this business, too?"

"My father left us when I was just six years old. We never heard from him again."

"That's too bad. I'm sorry to hear that," Mrs. Rock said.

"It's okay. We have done fine without him."

"Winter and I have been discussing ways to grow her business," Jonathan said. "We would like to rent a big enough space to have a store for their wares, a cafe, and a music venue all in one place."

"That's very ambitious," Mr. Rock said. "Once you've graduated from college and have your business degree, you will be prepared to accomplish that."

Jonathan winced slightly and glanced at Winter, who gave him a look that said, "Stand firm!"

"In the meantime," Mr. Rock said, "can we discuss the damage to the station wagon?"

"What damage?" Mrs. Rock asked. She and Winter both looked at Jonathan.

"There's a dent in the wood on the rear side panel," Jonathan said. He glanced at Winter, whose eyes softened. "Someone must have hit me in the parking lot. I'll pay to repair it."

"Yes, you will. You'll also need money for a car because you won't be using your mother's anymore," Mr. Rock said. His face flushed with anger.

"Fine, I'll keep that in mind," Jonathan said, controlling his own building temper. He breathed deeply before continuing. "Back to our ideas for the store. I don't want to wait two more years before starting my life. That's what it feels like to me. I've thought about this very seriously for some time. I won't be returning to Bancroft in September. I need to start living my life now."

Silence emanated from his shocked parents. Mrs. Rock found her tongue first. "I don't understand. When do you plan to do this? Where will you live down there?"

"And what do you plan to do for money while you wait for this miracle of a store to materialize?" Mr. Rock asked. His sarcasm tainted the atmosphere of the room. He pushed his chair back from the table and stood. "This is ridiculous, Jonathan. I need to talk to you privately. Now!"

"Winter can hear anything you have to say," Jonathan said, remaining seated.

"It's okay." Winter stood. "I'll wait outside while you talk to your parents."

"I'm sorry about this, Winter," Mrs. Rock said softly.

"It's okay," Winter said, smiling sadly, and left.

Mr. Rock stood silently until the front door clicked shut,

then sat back down across from Jonathan. "Now, can we be a bit more realistic here? What exactly are you planning on doing?"

"As I said, I can't go back to Bancroft. The curriculum bores me, and I feel like I'm wasting my time there. Those two years of college won't go to waste. I've learned enough to help get this business going. Once I know what my goals are, I can continue with college later if I need to. But right now, the best place for me to be is on Cape Cod, with Winter. I have almost nine hundred dollars saved up. I can work extra shifts for the rest of the summer, save enough for a used car, and get a job on the Cape when I move there."

"Hang on! Slow down for a minute here!" Mr. Rock waved his hand in front of his face as if chasing away a fly. "You've known this girl for two weeks and been in her company for only a few days, as far as I can tell. But you're ready to turn your whole life upside-down because of her?"

"It's not just about Winter. I've been unhappy since I started college. I went to Bancroft to make you happy. You know I wanted to study music, but I gave in to your arguments about getting a degree in business." Jonathan paused to gather his breath and his thoughts. "I have to live my own life. I can't live yours. I can't live the life you think I should."

"You haven't lived long enough to know what you want," Mr. Rock said.

"Then I guess it's time I did," Jonathan said, angrily rising from the table. "Maybe I should start right now."

"Jonathan, wait, please!" Mrs. Rock pleaded. She held out her arms to him. "You can't just leave like this. And you can't just go live with some girl you just met. I'm sure her mother wouldn't want that either."

"Right," Mr. Rock added. "We don't know anything about her family other than their father abandoned them, and they sell Indian trinkets to tourists."

"You know what? This conversation is over!" Jonathan yelled. He turned his back on them and stormed down the hall.

"Wait, Jonathan!" Mrs. Rock called out.

"Let him go, Kathy. He'll be back soon enough when he comes to his senses." Mr. Rock drew his chair to the table. "I need to eat something before I go back to work."

WINTER LEANED against the VW bus, wondering how things were going with Jonathan and his parents. Then Jonathan walked out the front door, carrying his duffel bag, backpack, and guitar case. *Not so great, I guess.*

"I'll drive," he said. "If it's okay with you?"

Winter opened the side door so he could stow his things, gave him a quick hug, got into the passenger seat, and said, "Let's go."

9

SATURDAY, JUNE 22, 2047

"So you just left home and never went back?" I ask.

My grandfather looks confused for a moment, but as his eyes focus on mine, he smiles. "Well, I never went back permanently."

"That sounds like quite a story," comes a soft voice behind us.

I turn and see Amoon standing just inside the doorway.

"My grandfather is telling me how he met my grandmother seventy years ago."

Amoon comes into the room. "That is a beautiful carving you're holding. May I see it?" she asks. She reaches out her hands for the carved deer. She holds it up and studies it. "It is very detailed and life-like. I can feel the energy of the animal inside." She hands it back to Grandpa. "It must be very important to you."

"It led me to Winter, my late wife. I've told you about her."

"It is good that you still have it as a reminder of happy times. I'm sorry if I interrupted your story, but I wanted to see if you need anything. They will be bringing dinner soon."

I walk down the hall as Amoon administers to Grandpa's

needs. Images from his story flit through my brain as I envision my grandparents as twenty-year-old kids in love, way back in the 1970s. So much has changed since then, yet some things remain the same, like young people falling in love. I try not to think about Rafael cooking and laughing in the tiny kitchen in our apartment, his curly brown hair falling into his eyes.

When I return, my grandfather is sitting up in bed, looking out the window with half-closed eyes. He doesn't seem to notice my presence, so I say softly as I sit in the chair beside his bed, "Hi, Grandpa. I'm back."

He turns slowly towards me and manages a small smile but doesn't speak.

"Thank you for telling me that story," I say. "You were so brave to do what you did, to stand up for yourself and just leave, without knowing how you'd make out or where you'd end up."

"I couldn't continue attending college just to make my parents happy. And I knew I would end up with Winter."

"Still, it took a lot of courage. I wish I had the nerve to quit my dead-end job and devote myself to writing full-time, but I can't. I need the money just to live."

"The only thing stopping you is yourself. I've just told you how I changed my life. You can, too. There's no reason why you can't work and write in your free time. Your grandmother would want you to follow your dreams. She loved reading your poems and stories."

"I shouldn't make excuses, Grandpa. But you had Grandma, and I have no one. I thought Rafael and I would be partners for life, but that didn't happen. I'm not even sure I can keep my apartment now that I have to pay all the bills." My voice cracks with emotion, and tears fill my eyes.

Grandpa leans over and touches my hand, his eyebrows drawn together. "I'm sorry, Luna. You're right. I'll never know what would have happened if I hadn't met Winter, but I like to think I still would have chosen to live my life my way."

I take a deep breath and wipe my eyes. "I know I have to get my act together and climb out of this rut I'm stuck in. I go to work, come home, grab some dinner, pour myself a glass of wine, and watch TV until I fall asleep."

I hesitate and bite my lip, trying to decide if I should say more. "Actually, I usually drink more than one glass of wine. Rafael drank a lot, and I learned to drink along with him. It didn't seem to be a problem then, but it's become a habit I can't break. It's the only thing that takes away the stress." I lower my head into my hands as tears fall again.

Grandpa rubs my shoulder and says quietly, "It's nothing to be ashamed of. The fact that you're aware of the problem and can admit it is the first step. You should talk to your mother. Soleil is very understanding. Maybe you could go back home to live for a while. Being alone doesn't help."

"I'll think about talking to my mom, but I don't want to move back home. I'm proud that I've made it on my own, so far."

"I wonder where you get that from?" he says, smiling. "But please ask for help if you need it."

"I will, Grandpa, I promise. You're right—being alone doesn't help, but drinking alone is the real problem. I'm going to start there." I kiss him on the cheek. "I'm going to get going now. I'll see you tomorrow."

IT'S a short trip from the elder home to my grandfather's house. As I drive through the woods down the last, narrow, winding road that lets out onto the beach road, I see movement to my right. A white-tailed doe leaps between the trees beside me. I slow down to a crawl and watch as she stops to stare at me with big brown eyes. Then she turns and springs into the woods. I continue on my way, feeling strangely calm and comforted by the sight of the doe.

I park my car in the driveway in back of my grandfather's house. No charging port here, but it's got plenty of juice. The house is set with its front facing the beach, pushing into the dunes. The sand falls away along its sides so that the back of the house shows four levels, with the basement exposed. The back basement door is the most accessible entry. The sand, year after year, creeps steadily towards the front and sides of the house, making it difficult to go up the side pathway to the front door. The path has all but disappeared under sand and long beachgrass. I'll put that on the list of *Things to be fixed*.

I look up at the house. The blue-gray paint is faded and peeling. When I enter the basement, which contains a small bedroom and bathroom, a strong, musty smell assaults me, indicating a possible mold problem. Paint and mold: two more items for the list, although we don't have to paint the house to rent it. I am determined to convince the family, primarily my mom and Aunt April, that renting rather than selling would be easier and perhaps as cost-effective.

After unpacking, I open the windows to let in fresh air, then do some quick dusting and sweeping in the rooms I'll use. Then, I kick off my shoes and head out for a nice long beach walk.

Extreme weather and erosion have also shifted sand onto the path from the front door to the beach, pushing the dunes up against the house, and forming a wall that drops off sharply to the waterfront. Some homeowners on the beach contract with companies that move and replace sand and build protective barriers, but this work is expensive and not guaranteed to last. That's another downside of selling an oceanfront home, but it wouldn't deter people from renting it for a week or two.

I reach the water's edge and ask myself the traditional question: *left or right?* Either direction allows for a walk of over a mile before having to turn back. I choose left, shut down my mind, listen to the sound of the waves, allow the cold water to tickle my feet, and walk. Kids play by the water's edge, fishermen surf cast lazily, and couples walk hand in hand, smile, and say hello to all they pass. I occasionally look down at the shells and worn rocks, to see if any heart-shaped ones jump out at me. My grandma always told me not to look too closely, or I wouldn't find one. She said you have to let them find you.

The beach has always been my happy place, generated over a lifetime of trips to my grandparents' house in all seasons. Even though we always lived in Vermont, my parents and I would come down here at least once a month throughout the year and more often in the summer. Sometimes, when I was little, my parents would leave me with my grandparents for a week or two while they took a trip together or to allow me my own little getaway. When I became a teenager and didn't need babysitting anymore, I still came down to visit and stay for my own vacation, especially in the summer.

I come to an inlet, forcing me to turn around and go back. My legs are getting tired, but it feels so good to be outside walking that I don't care. When I return, I will relax and have a light dinner of cheese, crackers, fruit, and seltzer. There's a bottle of wine in the car, but I purposely left it there.

I'm almost back at my grandfather's house when I spot a few young guys in front of the house next door. They have built a circular fire pit with beach rocks and are piling wood in it. They've set up chairs and small tables around the fire pit. One of them waves to me and jogs down to meet me. He has shaggy blond hair, blue eyes, and a handsome, friendly face. He wears what I can only think of as old-fashioned California surfer clothes—long flower print swim trunks and a faded-out, orange tee shirt with the sleeves cut off. It's easy to admire his well-muscled, tanned arms.

"Hi! Are you staying in the house next door? We were wondering if anyone was there."

"Just overnight. It's my grandfather's house, but he lives in an elder care home now, so I stay here when I visit him."

"My name's Adam, Adam Foster," he says, placing his right hand over his heart. "It's nice to meet you."

"Hi, I'm Luna. It's nice to meet you, too."

"Luna, like the moon?"

I laugh. "Yes, like the moon."

"Well, Luna, you are welcome to join our little Summer Solstice party here. We have plenty of food and drinks. It's just me and two friends and whoever else wanders by. Come over any time."

I hesitate for a moment. My walk has refreshed me, and this guy's friendly, open face revives my spirit. The thought of staying alone in the musty house while my neighbors have fun around a fire on the beach is depressing.

"Okay," I say before I can talk myself out of it. "I'll come down in a little while. I'll bring some munchies and a bottle of wine."

"Great, see you soon!" he says, heading back to his friends.

I retrieve the bottle of white wine from the car and put it in the fridge to chill. After showering and changing into jeans and a fancier tee shirt, I arrange my light dinner items on a colorful old platter of my grandmother's. I take the wine from the fridge and chase away any second thoughts about socializing with people I don't even know. Remembering Adam's friendly smile encourages me to head out to the beach.

Adam and his friends, Scott and Miguel, are from Boston, where they work for a renewable energy company. They arrived at the house today for a two-week rental. Eventually, Scott and Miguel stroll down the beach, where there is room to play with their mini drones, zooming them up and down the beach.

Adam and I chat. He tells me about his job, which includes maintaining solar panels and wind turbines.

"What do you do, Luna?"

"I work for a publishing company in Boston. I love books. I also consider myself a writer, although I have yet to publish anything."

"Well, you work in the right place for it!"

"That's true," I say. "Right now, I'm mostly concerned about saving my grandfather's house from being sold to pay for the elder home. I hope to convince the rest of the family to rent it rather than sell it. Do you mind telling me how much you're paying to rent this house?"

He gives me a higher number than I expect to hear. I'll have to do some math and contact a real estate agent to complete my research, but this makes me more optimistic. I also ask Adam if he knows anything about erosion reconstruction companies, and he promises to get me more information. The conversation flows smoothly between us. I am feeling surprisingly optimistic about this guy, too. He seems genuine.

I check my phone; it's after ten. I'd love to stay and keep talking, but I should head in to get some sleep. I have to get up early tomorrow and catch up on sleep after staying up so late last night. I'm tired but content, happy with myself for having drunk only two glasses of wine interspersed with seltzer. Adam doesn't appear to be a heavy drinker—he's had only a few beers all evening—another plus for this possible relationship.

"I have to head for home," I say, pulling myself out of the low beach chair.

He reaches for my hand and helps me up. "Okay, Let me walk you home," he says, keeping my hand in his as we head to the house.

We pause when we reach the door, and he turns to me and smiles. "Thank you so much for coming, Luna. You made it a party for me."

"Thanks for inviting me. I had fun. It was sure better than sitting around the house by myself."

"I wish you didn't have to leave tomorrow. Could you stay a little longer? I hope that doesn't sound too pushy, but I would like to get to know you better."

"That's okay. I feel the same way. But I have to visit my grandfather tomorrow and get back to Boston. Next week will be hectic. I have a project deadline before the end of the month."

Adam's face falls a little.

"But you know what?" I say. "I'll be back down for the Fourth of July, and you'll still be here. My whole family will be coming. We always have a big party on the Fourth. It's my grandfather's favorite holiday. You can come and meet him."

I don't mention that there is some controversy in the family about whether or not my grandfather should come to the house, especially if they decide to sell it.

"That sounds like a plan! I can't wait!" Adam says. He gives me a hug, which I return. He gives me a kiss, too, quick but firm, releases me, and walks away smiling.

I feel better than I have in months.

10

SUNDAY, JUNE 23, 2047

Sunlight and cool morning air pour through the open bedroom windows and wake me at six. I climb out of bed, ready to work on my list of reasons not to sell the house. I recall the events of the evening before. Adam's blue eyes and easy smile keep flashing in my brain. I can't stop thinking about him as I grab some fruit for breakfast. I dust and sweep my way around the house, making notes as I go. I should have asked Adam to meet me for a walk on the beach this morning.

Happy memories fill every corner of this old house. The bright, country-style kitchen where I would help my grandmother cook and bake occupies the back of the main floor of the house. Colorful clay bowls and platters line the counters. The large wooden table, handmade by Grandma's brother, Willy, patiently waits for a crowd of hungry people to sit, eat, talk, and enjoy one another's company. It is scarred with decades of dings, stains, and scratches, but the rich wood still glows after years of hand-polishing. If we sell the house, all this will have to be removed. But if we rent, we can leave most of it for the tenants' use.

The cozy living room takes up the middle of the house, with

a stone fireplace as its centerpiece. Comfortable chairs and a couch are set around it, with woven pillows thrown here and there. Floor-to-ceiling bookshelves hold everything from modern poetry to Shakespeare, Stephen King to F. Scott Fitzgerald, atlases, dictionaries, and books about Cape Cod and the Wampanoag. Old-fashioned board games like Monopoly, Life, Sorry, checkers, chess, and backgammon lie in haphazard stacks. I dust and straighten out everything the best I can. It would be easier to leave most of this for the enjoyment of renters, rather than have to pack it all up and either store it or sell it.

I continue to the front porch, which overlooks the beach. In the summer, screens replace the glass windows to allow the sea breeze in, making the porch an ideal place to sleep on hot summer nights. The windows haven't been removed yet this year, so it is like an oven out here. A large crack runs down the center of one of the windows, which I make a note of. The porch door leads to the beach path, now partly obscured by sand dunes. I open the door and step outside to check the front of the house. It's even more worn and in need of painting than the back due to the assault of wind and sand from the beach and the ocean. It would look better with a new coat of paint, but being cosmetic, that's probably not essential for either sale or rent.

On the second floor, my bedroom and the bathroom are pretty clean, so I dust and sweep the other two bedrooms. It's strange to see the master bedroom missing the dresser and other furniture that now occupy Grandpa's room at the elder home. The big four-poster bed still stands in the center of the room, and several watercolor paintings remain on the walls.

The closet has been emptied except for a few of my grand-mother's items that we haven't had the heart to part with. Skirts, dresses, and blouses covered with detailed beadwork done by her and my great-grandmother hang there. I remove one of the blouses to wear later. I wonder if I should find a better place for the rest of the items. Maybe the Cape Rocks Emporium would be interested in taking them. Some of the staff are relatives of my grandmother, and they have a room devoted to displaying Indigenous crafts. I'll drop by on my way to the elder home and ask.

I climb the stairs to the third floor, an attic turned into a bedroom of sorts on one side and an office workspace on the other. Closed up like the front porch, it also feels like an oven. *Has anyone been up here since Grandma died?* Everything, including the wood floor, is covered with a thick layer of dust. The bedroom side contains five mismatched twin beds, with two folded cots leaning against the angled walls. My grandparents ensured there were enough beds for all their family and friends to stay at any time. When they set up this room, they probably anticipated more grandchildren.

On the office and workspace side facing the beach, an extra-large dormer window allows for a spectacular ocean view. I open it to let fresh air into the hot, musty space. A cushioned bench is built into the window. I used to cozy up on it to read or look out over the water. A desk faces this window, where Grandpa did paperwork and wrote songs. Grandma drew, painted, or worked here on her many crafts. An old laptop and piles of books and papers cover the top of the dusty desk and spill over onto the floor.

A pile of necklaces and bracelets rests on top of a cardboard box pushed to the back of the desk. I pick them up to inspect them, then step back in surprise. My name, *Luna,* is written in red marker on the box. *This is like finding buried treasure!* I remove the tape and open the box.

An envelope rests on top, with my name written in my grandmother's flowing cursive. I place the letter on the desk to open later. Under it lie an object wrapped in fabric, three perfect heart-shaped rocks, more intricately beaded jewelry, smooth pieces of blue sea glass, and a small wooden box. Neatly bundled piles of crumbling, yellowed letters, an old photo album, and a folder of hand-written sheet music fill the bottom of the box.

I unwrap the cloth from the first item to reveal a carved wooden deer—a doe—a perfect mate to my grandfather's buck and an exact likeness of the deer I saw yesterday. Next, I open the small wood box to find my grandmother's engagement ring, an oval stone of smooth, purple wampum embedded in the center of a silver band. She had taught me, with great reverence, about the significance of wampum to the Wampanoag. This had been her grandmother's ring: another treasure. I glance through the photo album, letters, and hand-written sheet music. I'll wait until I have more time to savor them. One of them is the musical score and lyrics for "Waiting for Winter." I put it on top of the pile.

I look at my grandmother's letter and hesitate. I feel she is here with me, looking over my shoulder, waiting for me to open it. "Okay, Grandma," I say out loud and open it. I read it slowly, savoring the sound of her calm, warm voice in my head. Phrases leap off the page: "I hope this will help you care for the house...It may be of some value...I know you love this little piece of Cape Cod as much as we do...Follow your dreams...I love you and will always be with you."

My eyes blur as I read and reread the letter. I miss her so much. When she died at the end of my junior year in college, I was devastated and depressed. I consoled myself by writing down memories of my times with her. Someday, I intend to compile them into a book. I used the stories for my senior thesis, but I've never published them, The material is too private, too personal.

My hands shake as I read the letter one more time. I'm suddenly breathless in the hot, stuffy attic. I sit, put my head down on the dusty desk, and cry. I cry for the loss of my grandmother, for the state of my grandfather's health, and for the difficult decisions that need to be made about the house.

Eventually, I calm myself and repack the box. As I place the letter on top, the words "It may be of some value" replay in my mind. *What may be of some value? The ring? The deer? The sheet music?* I'll look through everything again later, but for now, I have to get out of this suffocating room. I pick up the box and head downstairs.

I put the box on the kitchen table and head outside to the beach to clear my head. The soft sand under my bare feet has warmed under the morning sun. I head to the water's edge, breathing in that familiar salty air, and allow the rhythm of the waves to soothe me as they break softly over my toes. I reach down, cup my hands, scoop up the cool water, and splash it on my face.

Grandma's words linger in my mind, "Take care of the house. I know you love it." *Maybe this is where I belong, but how do I make that happen?* I become more resolved than ever to keep this house from being sold, no matter what. I need to talk to my grandfather. It's wrong to keep him in the dark about his financial situation. I'll tell him about the box and the letter and see if he knows which item "may be of some value."

A FRIENDLY VOICE calls from the road as I load my things into the car. "Hey, Luna, that's a nice car!" It's Adam, riding a fat tire bike down the driveway. He sounds and looks just as good as he did last night.

"Thanks. My dad works for a new electric car dealership, so he got me a good deal."

"That's a pretty shirt, too."

"It was my grandmother's. She probably beaded it herself. It smells a little musty, but I feel close to her today, so I wanted to wear it. The sea breeze will freshen it." I don't have time to tell Adam about the box. Right now, I'm reluctant to.

"Are you leaving now?"

"Yes, I'm going to visit my grandfather at the elder home, then head back to Boston. I'm stopping at the Cape Rocks Emporium first. Have you been there? It's up on Route 6A. My grandparents started that business a long time ago."

"I haven't been there, but I've passed by it a few times. I'll check it out soon." He rummages in his back pocket for his device. "I know you said you'd be down for the Fourth of July, but can we exchange numbers? I forgot to ask last night."

"Of course," I say. He holds his device up to mine, and we have each other's numbers. That feels good.

I PULL into the last available space in the parking lot of the Cape Rocks Emporium, a large barn-red building. People gather around picnic tables in the backyard area, engaged in a basket-weaving class. A woman sits off to the side, in front of a group of children, playing guitar and leading them in a sing-a-long. Customers sit around the bistro tables on the front patio, chatting and enjoying coffee and pastries.

A life-sized wooden bear holds a *Welcome* sign next to the entrance. Colorful displays of paintings, books, and Indigenous crafts fill the window displays. Posters advertising music events, lectures, and workshops are tacked around the front door. I notice an advertisement for a class to learn the Wampanoag language. My grandmother had told me how it had been lost for over one hundred years. Then, in the 1990s, a tribal woman experienced recurring dreams in which her ancestors spoke to her in Wampanoag, and she championed its return for the rest of her life.

I enter the Emporium and am surrounded by the warm,

inviting aromas of coffee and baked goods. I walk through the cafe area to the craft goods area. I look around at the handmade pottery, baskets, jewelry, carved wooden figures, paintings, and clothing. A young woman wearing an intricately beaded red cotton dress speaks with the customers, explaining the various pieces. She glances my way and smiles broadly. She excuses herself and approaches me with open arms.

"Luna! It's so good to see you!" she says as she embraces me.

"It's good to see you too, Aria," I respond. I step back to admire her dress and the beaded bracelets, necklaces, and earrings that enhance her attractiveness. Her features and coloring are a mix of African, Indigenous, and European, but she always maintains that, regardless of DNA percentages, she is all Wampanoag.

Aria is a third or fourth cousin of mine. We've never figured out the exact kinship term to use, but we share a great-great-grandmother, as she is the granddaughter of my great-grand-mother's sister, Elizabeth. Too complicated, so we always just call ourselves cousins. We played together as kids, but she's a few years older, so things changed once she was a teenager. However, we've remained friendly and have seen each other often over the years.

"That has to be one of Aunt Winter's blouses," she says.

"It is, and it's one of the reasons I'm here. I need to clear out personal items from the house. Would you be interested in having some things to display or sell? There is clothing, jewelry, baskets, and other little knick-knacks. You could take a look when you come for the Fourth and take whatever you want."

"I'll take anything you're giving away," Aria says. She hesitates before adding, "Is there a reason you're clearing things out? How's Uncle Jonathan doing?"

"He's weakening physically, but his mind is fairly intact. The elder home is very costly, so we might have to rent the house."

"That's too bad, but okay, as long as you can keep it in the family. It would be so sad to lose that house."

"That's how I feel, too," I say and hug Aria goodbye.

I ARRIVE at the elder home at ten-thirty and head inside, with the wooden doe, the wampum ring, and Grandma's letter stashed in my tote bag. I peek into my grandfather's room. He is still in bed, apparently sleeping. That seems odd for this time of day. The caretakers usually get him up and out of bed by now, even if it's against his will.

An aide sees me hesitate at the door. He waves and walks over.

"Hello, are you here to see Mr. Rock? He's been very tired today. We got him up for breakfast, but afterward, he said he wanted to go back to bed."

"I'm his granddaughter, Luna. Is he alright? Should I wake him?"

"Hello, Luna. It's nice to meet you. I'm Marco," the aide says, smiling and putting his right hand over his heart in greeting. "I don't think anything is wrong. He's fatigued and worn down. The doctor will check on him later. For now, I think the best thing would be to wake him up so he can spend some time with his granddaughter."

"Okay, thank you, Marco, I'll do that."

I walk into the room quietly and watch him sleep for a bit, thinking again how strong and handsome he looks through all the lines and wrinkles of age. It's probably my fault he's so tired. He did a lot of talking yesterday. Maybe I shouldn't bring up the subject of money problems yet and let him rest. I hate to disturb him, but he would be mad if I didn't wake him, so I sit beside his bed and put my hand on his arm.

"Hey, Grandpa, wake up. It's Luna," I say quietly, lightly

rubbing his arm until he stirs and opens his eyes. It takes a moment for him to recognize me, but he gives me that loving glance that melts my heart.

"How are you feeling? Marco said you were so tired this morning you had to go back to bed after breakfast. Are you okay?"

"Who's Marco?"

"The aide on duty this morning. The man with dark curly hair?"

"I don't know him. But I'm okay. Just tired."

"Did you sleep well last night?"

"I don't know how I slept," he growls. "Stop asking me so many questions." He waves his hands in front of his face.

"I'm sorry. It's okay. Let's get you out of bed, and I'll take you outside to the patio. It's a beautiful day out there—not too hot."

He calms himself, putting his hands down shakily on the bed. "Okay, that sounds good. I'm sorry for being cranky. It's so nice of you to visit me. Weren't you just here not too long ago?"

"I was here yesterday. I stayed at the house last night and came back today."

"What house?"

"Your house, Grandpa. Your house on the beach." I begin to worry about how 'out of it' he seems. Since his stroke, he's had occasional episodes of forgetfulness and confusion, but they're usually short-lived. I hope he just needs some fresh air and company to revive him. He looks at me, then around the room, as if to reorient himself. Then he looks back at me and reaches for my hand, which I clasp in mine.

"Of course, you stayed at my house," he says at last. "How does it look?"

"Pretty good. Let's get you out of bed, and I'll tell you about it. Let me get someone to help you."

I press the call button on the remote. I see something under the blanket. I lift it to find the wooden deer. I pick it up and put it on the nightstand.

"My deer!" I thought I lost it."

"No, it's right here. And I have a surprise for you. I'll show you once we're outside."

I WAIT in the lobby until Marco wheels my grandfather out and tells me he'll serve us lunch on the patio. I notice the deer is tucked into the wheelchair by Grandpa's side. We sit at a shaded table in a small alcove surrounded by potted plants and flowers with a view of Cape Cod Bay. Large fans stand at intervals to ward off the summer heat, but they are not needed yet today. Grandpa has perked up, happy to be in the open air.

"I told you I had a surprise. Are you ready?" I say, opening my bag.

"I haven't had a surprise in a long time," he says happily.

I remove the wooden doe and hold it up for him to see.

His eyes brighten. "That's Winter's doe! Where did you find it?"

I tell him about the box but don't mention the letter yet. When I show him the wampum ring, he is quiet for a minute, his eyes looking back to the past.

"I can't believe we never found that box before now, but I haven't been up to the attic in a long time." He pauses and looks wistfully out to sea, his eyes moistening. "I miss that house."

"I can't imagine how much you must miss it. But at least the deer are back together." I place the doe next to the buck on the table. "Yesterday, I saw a doe like this in the woods on the way to your house."

"Of course—she's watching over you. That's right—I was telling you the story about the deer and Winter. I have to finish it."

"That's okay—I think I know the rest of the story," I say, intrigued by the notion of the deer watching over me. "You and Grandma got married, had your three children, opened up the Cape Rocks Emporium, and ended up having the best granddaughter in the world!"

He laughs and says, "Yes, but I need to tell you more, especially after seeing the wooden doe and the ring again."

"Okay, but I don't want you to get tired from talking. Just tell me the important parts. What happened after you left home and went to the Cape with Grandma?"

"I spent the rest of the summer living in a storage room at The General Store. Noah set up a cot for me, and I worked in the store to repay him, even though he didn't really need extra help. I went to Winter's house to wash up, and I ate with them from time to time. My relationship with Willy was still strained, but he had quit drinking whiskey after the incident in July. He was okay as long as he just stuck to beer."

"That must have been hard on you, going from living in your parents' nice house to living in a storage room."

"Honestly, it was tough. I had more than one moment of doubt. Then I'd see Winter, and they'd vanish. Also, I never had any regrets about quitting Bancroft. I missed some of my musician friends from back home, but I had my guitar and figured I'd eventually see them again and make new friends on the Cape.

"Once September came, Winter and I rented a small summer cottage. It wasn't winterized, so we had to heat it with electric heaters. Mary and Willy were not completely comfortable with the arrangement, but we discussed it and got their guarded approval before moving in together. I got a regular job at a supermarket in Hyannis and bought a beat-up old Chevy pickup truck to get around in."

"What about your parents? Did you talk to them?"

"My father and I barely spoke, but I called my mother once

a week to check in. She was always more accepting. Winter and I went for dinner on Christmas Day. It was awkward but relatively cordial. I also took a few trips home now and then to visit my friends."

"Well, that must have been a tough winter to get through."

"It certainly was. Did you ever hear of the Blizzard of '78?"

11

———

MONDAY, FEBRUARY 6, 1978

"It's really coming down out there!"

"Are you guys closing early?"

"They didn't say it was going to be this bad!"

Jonathan listened to the customers' comments about the weather as he rang up their emergency supplies of milk, bread, cereal, Pop-Tarts, potato chips, Ring Dings, Devil Dogs, and whatever else they felt was necessary to survive the storm. He glanced out the large window behind him between customers, monitoring the conditions outside. The snow fell rapidly and heavily, but the wind was the real culprit, blowing so strongly that visibility was impossible.

The snowstorm had been predicted, but the Cape was often spared large amounts of snow because of the warmer ocean surrounding it. This winter, however, the Cape had already received several more inches of snow than average. The electric wires around Jonathan and Winter's cottage did not hold up well in high winds, and they'd already been without electricity a few times. They didn't consider this a hardship, though. It was an opportunity to light candles and snuggle together under warm blankets.

That morning, Jonathan had dropped Winter off to work at her mother's house, about a mile from their cottage, before heading for Hyannis to his job. Over the winter months, the family was building up their stock of arts and crafts for the summer season. Jonathan and Winter still planned to rent space where they could open their dream store, cafe, and music venue. All they needed was the space and the money, and they'd be all set. Easier said than done, but he worked as many hours as he could, saving as much money as possible.

A couple of employees asked the manager if he would close early due to the storm. "Not as long as people are still coming in," he said. "We need to stay open for them. If nobody comes in for a whole hour, maybe we'll close."

The number of customers had dropped to a trickle by seven, but they kept straggling in, so the store didn't close until nine. Given the ferocity of the storm, a few employees decided to stay put at the store until the weather calmed down, but Jonathan had to head home to Winter. He couldn't call her since neither the cottage nor Mary's house had a telephone.

He stashed an emergency can of Coke and a bag of nuts in his coat pockets before stepping out into the howling wind. He shielded his face with the hood of his coat. It was quite a trek to his truck, parked at the far end of the lot. He pushed his way through the foot-plus of snow already on the ground. The wind drove tiny, icy snowflakes into his face.

Finally at the truck, he found the snow piled in packed drifts halfway up the driver's side door. He used his mittened hands as shovels to clear enough of it away to open the door and climbed into the driver's seat. The old pickup started up with a roar on the first turn of the key, and Jonathan let out a whoop of victory. He let the motor run, put the heat on, and got out to clean off the windshield and dig more snow out from around the tires. Then he put the truck into low gear and fishtailed out of the parking lot to the main road. It was mostly empty, even of town plows.

It took all his concentration to negotiate the roads. The snow whirled so thick it was all he could do to see the road. Several cars were parked along the sides, and Jonathan looked for passengers inside as he passed. He was willing to stop to help someone if needed, but the cars all appeared to have been abandoned. A few vehicles still moved at a snail's pace along the snow-covered roads, mostly trying to avoid sliding into each other. The storm turned the half-hour trip home into almost two hours, and it was after eleven when Jonathan arrived in Mashpee.

Now he had to decide. Mary's house was on the way to the cottage. *Should I stop there first? Or should I go straight home?* It made sense to stop at the Jones' house first. *Winter might have stayed there to wait out the storm.*

He almost drove past the small street, obscured by the driving snow and wind. He couldn't afford to get the pickup stuck, so he pulled over as far as possible, put on the four-way flashers, and made his way down the road on foot, carrying a flashlight to guide him. The electricity was out. The houses he passed were dark and barely visible in the storm, with the occasional flickering of candles inside breaking the blackness.

No candles glowed from the windows of the Jones' house. *It's late. They probably went to bed.* Jonathan pushed his way through the snow to the front door. *I hope I don't scare them.*

Suddenly, Max let out a long stream of ferocious barking from inside. The door flew open, and Willy appeared, holding Max back by the collar. "Stay back!" he yelled. "Get the hell out of here!"

Jonathan stopped at the bottom of the steps and turned the flashlight toward the ground. "Willy, it's me, Jonathan."

Willy pulled Max into the house. "What are you doing here? Where's Winter? Is she okay?"

"I just got here from work. I thought she might still be here. Can I come in for a minute?"

Willy turned without a word and let Jonathan into the pitch-black house. Jonathan used his flashlight to guide them to the kitchen. He took off his coat and gloves and shook them out. Shivering, he realized how cold it was inside. Willy was wearing his winter coat and woolen hat. He lit a candle, and they sat at the table.

"Willy? What's going on?" Mary called from behind her bedroom door.

"It's okay. It's Jonathan. Stay in bed. It's too cold out here."

"What? No, I'll come out," she said. She appeared a minute later, a blanket wrapped around her heavy coat, a wool hat on her head, and a candle in her hand.

"Jonathan, why are you here? Is Winter alright?" she asked, sitting at the table.

Willy answered for him. "He's just getting home from work. He thought Winter might still be here."

Turning to Jonathan, he added, "Winter insisted on going home before the storm got too bad. The power was still on at that point, or I would have insisted she stay here."

Willy's tone took on a sinister edge. "You need to get over there right now and make sure she's okay. I don't know what you think you're doing with my sister. It's not all fun and games around here, you know. Sometimes, I think you're just playing house. Winter deserves better than that."

Jonathan hesitated before replying. He wasn't about to start an argument with Willy under the current conditions. He needed to get home to Winter. The wind outside howled and whistled around the window panes. He looked at Mary to see her reaction to Willy's words, but she remained silent, looking down at the table. The soft candlelight brought out the lines on her face. That Mary and Willy doubted his intentions with Winter troubled him deeply. He closed his eyes and rubbed his hands down his face, which still tingled with cold.

"I love Winter," he said at last, looking just as intently into Willy's eyes through the near darkness. "We're not just playing house. We're trying to build a life together." He turned to Mary. "You understand that, don't you?"

"I can see that you have deep feelings for one another, but you are so young. You hardly knew each other before moving in together. Like Willy, I do not want to see Winter get hurt," Mary replied softly.

Jonathan looked into her dark eyes, flickering in the tiny flame, trying to see things from her perspective. It was true that his and Winter's relationship had turned serious very swiftly. He knew how committed he was to her, and he was sure of Winter's commitment to him. But how could he—they—prove it to her mother and brother? He came to a decision and braced himself for his next words.

"I'll be twenty-one years old on Wednesday. Winter is twenty-one already. We are young—I give you that. But I love Winter and want to be with her for the rest of my life."

He swallowed hard. "Will you both give me your permission to ask her to marry me?"

Mary and Willy stared wide-eyed at him. Jonathan looked back and forth between them. He couldn't read their expressions in the low glimmer of the candles, but Willy's mouth had dropped open. Mary struggled to keep her lips from trembling. The rattle of the window panes in the wind was the only sound in the otherwise quiet kitchen.

Finally, Mary's face lit up in the candlelight. She reached across the table and clasped Jonathan's hand. "I trust my daughter's judgment. If Winter says yes, I will have another son." She beamed.

They both looked at Willy, whose face was a mask of surprise and confusion. At last, he found his tongue. "I stand behind whatever my mother says. She's the boss," he said. He broke into a smile, rose from the table, and stepped forward to give Jonathan a bear hug. Jonathan returned the embrace from his future brother-in-law.

Mary laughed, then turned serious, "I have one more thing to say. If you and Winter are to be married, we must arrange a meeting with your parents. Whatever your problems are with them, it troubles me that they disapprove of your living here. I cannot help but feel that they also disapprove of my family. We must clear the air between us."

"I agree," Jonathan said. "I promise I will speak to my parents."

"Thank you. When will you ask Winter?"

"I'd do it right now if I could, but I guess I should get a ring first."

Mary brightened. "Wait here. I have something for you." She picked up the candle and returned to her bedroom.

The two men sat staring at each other, listening to the storm roar outside. They were both curious about what Mary went to fetch.

"I wish I could offer you a shot of whiskey," Willy said at last, "but I've sworn off that for a while."

"No problem."

Mary returned with a small box and opened it. Inside was a silver ring embedded with a large, oval purple stone. As she removed the ring, Jonathan got a glimpse of a large gold coin underneath. Mary quickly grasped the coin and tucked it into her coat pocket.

"This was my mother's ring," she said, showing it to Jonathan and Willy in the dim light. "It is wampum, made from the shell of the quahog clam. The Wampanoag people consider wampum a sacred substance." She placed the ring back in the box and held it out to Jonathan. "I pass it on to you and Winter. It will honor our family and bring blessings to your marriage."

OH SHIT! What have I just got myself into?

Jonathan maneuvered the pickup through the still-raging storm. A riotous mix of thoughts filled his head: the decision he had just made to ask Winter to marry him, the promise to Mary about arranging a meeting with his parents, the extra responsibilities he had just taken on. *Well, there's only one way to go, and that is forward.*

At the moment, going forward through the slippery snow and fierce wind was a far greater challenge. It was well past midnight before he made it to the cottage. The truck had barely made it, sliding over roads that hadn't seen a plow for hours. He had to ram it through the ridge of snow in front of the cottage. Some of it had been piled there from a long-past plow, and the driving snow had built up into a hard drift. He trudged to the front door, full of a strange mixture of exhaustion and excitement, of uncertainty and confidence.

Taking a deep breath, he quietly opened the door and slipped into the darkness inside. His body was numb from the icy cold and wetness of the storm. He removed his coat and hat and draped them on the back of a chair. His boots and mittens dropped snow onto the floor near the door. In stocking feet, he tiptoed into the bedroom, where faint ambient light from the window showed a mountain of blankets on the bed. He opened the dresser drawer and felt around for dry clothes. As he pulled out sweatpants, two knit shirts, and thick socks, a rustling sound came from the direction of the bed.

"Jonathan?"

"Hi, I'm home. Sorry I'm so late. It's horrible out there," he said, turning on the flashlight.

"I was so worried. I thought maybe you were stuck at the store," Winter said, shoving the blankets aside as if to get up.

"Stay there. It's too cold in here," Jonathan said as he

quickly changed. He lit two candles, put them on the bedside table, and sat on the edge of the bed next to the mound that was Winter. She reached her hands out to him, and he leaned down for a long kiss.

"I stopped at your mom's house on the way back because I thought you might still be there."

"I wanted to get back here before the storm got too bad. Then the electricity went out. Was the power out there, too?"

"Yes, it was," Jonathan said. He hesitated, gathering his courage. "Winter, I have something important to ask you."

"You know you can ask me anything." She sounded as serious as he felt. "What is it?"

Jonathan took Mary's box out of his pocket and opened it under the candle's glow. "Winter Jones, I love you and want to spend the rest of my life with you. Will you marry me?"

Winter's mouth fell open in shock as she looked from Jonathan to the ring. For a moment, he worried he had done the wrong thing. Then, her face widened into that beautiful, crooked-tooth smile, and she said, "Yes, Jonathan Rock. I will marry you."

He climbed under the blankets with her. As the howling wind and snow rattled the tiny cottage, the heat of their bodies, tangled together, kept them warm through the remainder of the storm.

12

___

SUNDAY, JUNE 23, 2047

"Hello, Mr. Rock? I have your lunches here for you," says an aide, who appears beside our table on the patio carrying a loaded tray.

"Time for a break," I say. Let's eat, and then you can finish this romantic story. I can't wait to hear more!"

The truth is, I can't stop picturing Rafael proposing to me in an alternate version of my life. I chase that image out of my mind and concentrate on eating and taking in the ocean view. The weather is cooperating so far today. The air has warmed, but the sea breeze is light and steady. Many residents and their guests eat lunch, chat, and laugh around us.

I notice that my grandfather has barely touched his food.

"Aren't you hungry, Grandpa? You've hardly eaten a thing."

"I'm not hungry, just thirsty," he says in a husky voice, sipping his ginger ale. "I want to tell you about our wedding."

"Okay, but take a couple more bites of your sandwich first," I say, worrying that he's wearing down from talking so much.

He nibbles at his sandwich and resumes his story. "The first order of business after we announced our engagement was to keep my promise to Mary and arrange a meeting with my parents."

"And how did that go?"

"Not too bad, although it was awkward at times. My parents, Mary, Winter, and I met for lunch at a restaurant in Plymouth." A light returns to his eyes and a sly smile spreads on his lips. "We thought it wise to save Willy for later.

"My parents were reserved but polite toward Mary. She made a positive impression by telling them how she had built her Wampanoag Wares business. Later, discussing wedding plans strained the conversation, but we worked our way through it.

"Winter and I picked Fourth of July weekend to get married, the first anniversary of our meeting. We wanted to incorporate Native tradition into the wedding and have the minister from the Old Indian Meeting House in Mashpee officiate. At first, we planned the ceremony to take place in the yard at Mary's house. I knew my mother would be upset I wasn't getting married in a Catholic church, but she was so relieved that I wouldn't be *living in sin* anymore, she accepted our plans."

"But didn't you get married on the beach at your house?" I ask, forgetting if I've heard that part of the story.

"Yes, we did. Our off-season rental agreement on the cottage ended in the middle of June, so we had to find someplace else to live. That added another snag to our wedding plans."

"How were you able to buy the house so quickly?"

"We didn't, not right away. We rented it. Our old friend Noah, from The General Store, found it for us. The owner was an older man who was not well. He didn't live on the Cape, and the house had fallen into disrepair. He rented it out cheaply to anyone who would take it. It was in pretty bad shape, but the fact that it was right on the beach kept people renting."

He shook his head with a little laugh. "It's funny. When Noah told me he knew of a house on the beach in East Sandwich we could afford to rent, the first thing I thought of was that guy who gave me a ride when I left Michelle's house the year before—Nick, his name was—funny I remember that. Anyway, he had invited me to stay at a house on the beach in East Sandwich. I've always wondered if it was the same house, that maybe the house had been calling to me."

"Are you finished, sir?" The waiter is back to clear our plates.

"Yes, I'm done," Grandpa says, pushing his plate away impatiently.

"So, you and Grandma moved into the house before the wedding?" I ask, making a mental note to talk to someone about his lack of appetite.

"We moved in the middle of June. I remember that day so clearly. We didn't have much to move since we were going from one furnished house to another, but Willy and Mary helped us transport our personal stuff. At the end of the day, we built a firepit on the beach and sat there, sipping wine and watching the sun go down. That's when Winter suggested we get married right there on the beach in front of the house. So we did, just three weeks later..."

13

SUNDAY, JULY 2, 1978

Jonathan inspected himself in the bathroom mirror in the basement. He had been exiled there by his mother and his future mother-in-law, who agreed that the groom should not see the bride before the wedding. So Jonathan had slept down there last night. The musty old mattress did not help in his fruitless efforts to sleep, conflicting joy and doubt spinning through his mind all night.

What the hell are you doing? he asked himself. *You're only twenty-one years old, have no money, no home of your own, a shaky job situation, and you're getting married?*

A vision of Winter came to his mind, her long dark hair flowing around her face, her crooked front teeth showing through that enigmatic smile. He remembered the day, exactly one year before, when he had first seen her at the flea market. Suddenly, an urge to hold the wooden deer nearly overwhelmed him, but it was upstairs in the bedroom he shared with Winter, from which he had been banished.

Jonathan took one more good look at himself in the mirror. He had combed out his long, thick, dark auburn hair neatly, and his face was clean-shaven. Mary Jones and her sisters had colorfully beaded, in record time, his light cotton shirt and pants. They fell comfortably around his tall, lean body. Winter would wear a similarly decorated dress. Their clothing was made of cotton rather than the traditional deerskin, but it resembled original Native wear. He wore leather sandals now, but they would be barefoot for the ceremony on the beach.

As expected, these last three weeks had been hectic—planning the ceremony, food, accommodations, and clothing, and settling into their new home. In the Wampanoag tradition, the bride and groom were expected to give presents to their guests instead of vice versa. Although Jonathan and Winter would accept gifts, with the help of Mary and her band of crafters, they had woven over forty small baskets and filled them with candy to hand out to the guests.

Jonathan's parents had arrived the previous night and came over in the morning from their hotel to help with the set-up. They were still uneasy about his and Winter's relationship, but even if they weren't very sociable or talkative, they remained polite and respectful toward Winter's family. Willy was on his best behavior, staying away from hard liquor and whatever pills they suspected he occasionally abused. He allowed himself—or Mary allowed him—to have a few beers during social gatherings.

Jonathan looked into his tawny brown eyes in the mirror, took three long, slow breaths, and smiled as he focused on thoughts of Winter. He might still doubt how the future would unfold, but he was sure he wanted to share it with her.

Finally, he made a few minor adjustments in the mirror and went to the bottom of the basement stairs. "Hey, I'm ready," he yelled to the floor above. "Can I come up now?"

~

THE WEDDING BEGAN with their version of a traditional Wampanoag marriage ceremony. Jonathan and the guests sat on folding chairs in a large circle on the beach in front of the house. A perfect summer day had unfolded for them—warm and breezy. The sun shimmered on the calm waves of Cape Cod Bay and seagulls cawed happily overhead.

Three musicians, all in colorful Native dress, sat on the sand outside the circle, softly beating their hide-covered drums. At a crescendo, the guests turned their attention to the flower-lined path leading from the house. Willy, resplendent in his intricately beaded deerskin suit, led Winter toward the circle.

Jonathan had not seen her since the previous night. He was struck anew by her unique beauty. She wore a red woven blanket over her beaded cotton dress. Her hair was brushed to a silky shine, and the ocean breeze played through it. A peaceful smile flickered around her lips; they trembled with emotion when she glanced at Jonathan. His heart beat so fast in his chest that he felt breathless. *You're okay—deep breaths,* he repeated over and over to himself.

When they arrived at the circle, Winter let go of Willy's arm. She smiled up at him as she stepped between her mother and aunt, seated opposite Jonathan, and walked to the center of the circle.

The beat of the drums shifted to a new pattern. Winter moved rhythmically around the inner circle, wrapping the blanket around herself. When she reached Jonathan, she stopped before him and opened the blanket. This was a sign of devotion to her new husband. She smiled, closed the blanket, stepped to the other side of the circle to her family, and opened the blanket again. This symbolized her continued loyalty to them.

The music changed once more as Winter paced across the circle directly to Jonathan. She spread the blanket on the ground at his feet and sat. Jonathan rose shakily from his chair and sat on the blanket beside her. Winter took his sweaty hand in hers and whispered in his ear, "It's okay. We are almost there." They rose, wrapping the blanket around them, to honor their eternal union. Together they stepped to the beat of the drums, back toward Winter's family, and exited the circle.

Now, the drummers put down their sticks, and Jonathan and Winter dropped the blanket and walked hand in hand back into the circle. The minister from the Old Indian Meeting House performed a short, traditional service. The bride and groom each said, "I do," and exchanged plain gold wedding bands. Finally, the minister said, "I now pronounce you man and wife. You may kiss the bride." They did so to the rousing applause of the guests.

Jonathan looked at his parents. His mother was wiping her eyes. He was happy his grandmother and aunt from New Jersey and a few friends from back home had been able to attend. The rest of the guests were family and friends from Winter's side.

The reception included a fully laden buffet table, drinks, music, dancing, and cake. Jonathan and Winter mingled with their families and friends, enjoying the jokes, teasing, and well wishes.

Noah, who had volunteered to be the photographer, another of his many talents, took pictures during the ceremony. Now, he wanted to capture individual shots of the couple and their family members. Gradually, he isolated each guest for an individual photo.

Eventually, he managed to pull Jonathan and Winter from the crowd and took them down the beach for some scenic photos. The couple welcomed a few moments to themselves. They were exhausted from the day. They chatted together, then walked silently for a spell, listening to the sounds of the party carried on the wind. The soft breaking of the waves on the sand beside them was soothing. Noah lagged behind to let them get ahead of him.

Away from the excitement, Jonathan and Winter put their arms around each other and settled down. They appeared happy and at peace, and Noah took advantage as they loosened up and relaxed. He took some shots of them walking away, then called out, "Hey, look at me!" When they turned, arms still around each other's waists, their smiling faces radiating pure happiness, Noah snapped the picture that captured forever that moment of joy, contentment, and excitement for whatever the future held.

As the sun dipped toward the sea, guests started to depart. A few stayed on to help clean up. Jonathan hugged his parents when they prepared to leave and promised to visit soon. After their departure, relief washed over him. The day had been a triumph on all fronts, with no major issues or conflicts. Willy had been on his best behavior, drinking just enough beer to keep him sociable. He had even danced with Jonathan's mother.

Now, Willy and Mary were the only guests left, and only one table remained on the beach. It held the wedding gifts: wrapped boxes, gift bags, and a basket full of cards.

"We should bring the gifts inside," Winter said. "It will be fun to open everything tomorrow. I don't have the energy for it now."

"But you have to open ours before we go!" Mary said. She poked Willy's arm. "Go find our presents."

Willie returned from the table with a long, cylinder-shaped package and a rectangular box wrapped in shiny gold paper. He handed the long cylinder to Jonathan. "This one is from my mother," he said.

Jonathan and Winter unwrapped it from either end, revealing a large cardboard tube. Winter reached inside and pulled out a rolled-up blanket. They shook it open and held it up. It was a woven blanket of red with symmetrical patterns of blue, yellow, and green.

"It's beautiful!" exclaimed Jonathan. He hugged Mary and Winter did the same. She held her mother in a long embrace. Tears in their eyes glinted in the last rays of the sun.

"My turn," said Willy, handing the box to Winter. "You open this one."

Winter carefully unwrapped the box and opened it. Inside was a solid item wrapped in tissue paper. She peeled away the paper to reveal a wood carving of a deer: a doe, a little smaller than Jonathan's buck. Its head was turned to the right, and its bright, realistic, brown eyes stared soulfully.

"Oh, Willy, thank you. It's amazing!" Winter exclaimed. She reached up to hug her brother.

"Thanks, Willy," Jonathan said, quickly embracing his new brother-in-law.

"You're welcome, brother," Willy said.

Night had fallen. Finally, they were alone. Jonathan and Winter took one last stroll to the water's edge and looked up at the stars. They held each other, their bare feet sinking into the cool, wet sand, the fresh night air blowing away any lingering doubts and worries about the future. They needed no words to share what emanated from their two hearts, which today had become one. Together they would face whatever came their way—the good and the bad. They had each other, and nothing else mattered...for now.

14

SUNDAY, JUNE 23, 2047

"What a beautiful wedding that must have been!" I say.

My grandfather's eyes mist over. The air has warmed a lot since lunch, and the outside fans have been turned on to refresh the remaining guests on the patio.

"When did you end up buying the house?"

"After April was born. In 1980. Money was extremely tight, but the owner had to sell, so he accepted our lowball offer. We still struggled financially. It was hard to keep the Wampanoag Wares business afloat while I worked at the supermarket and did odd jobs for extra money.

"I didn't want to ask my parents for help. They gave us a wedding gift of three hundred dollars. That went much farther back then but wasn't a significant amount of money. But it was funny. My father turned fifty soon after April was born, and between becoming a grandfather and having some kind of mid-life crisis, he gave us a gift of two thousand dollars. It was enough to help with a down payment on the house."

Talking about the house and money reminds me of the issue I've been avoiding. Now is as good a time as any to discuss the situation with his house. I run my hands through my hair and sigh. *Where do I start?*

"Is something wrong?" Grandpa asks, his frown lines deepening.

"Kind of," I say stupidly. Then I sit up straighter and look him in the eye. "It's hard for me to tell you this, but you need to know. The cost of this elder home is draining your finances. Mom and Aunt April have been looking for ways to use the house to help pay for it. One way would be to sell it, but I think we'd do fine if we just rented it instead."

He closes his eyes and rubs his hand over his forehead. "I see," he says in a whispery voice. He looks away from me, out toward the ocean. A tear slides down his cheek.

"Oh, Grandpa, I'm so sorry I had to bring this up. I promise you I won't let them sell your house. I've been working on ways to convince them that renting it would be a better option."

"I can't believe they'd even consider it," he says, turning back to me and wiping his eyes.

"Neither can I," I say.

"It seems the house isn't as important to my children as I'd hoped. None of them even stayed on the Cape. They all moved away."

"Maybe they take after their father," I say quietly, and place my hand over his on the arm of the wheelchair.

A weak smile spreads slowly across his face. "You've got me there, girl. But what about you, Luna? You always loved it here on the Cape. Winter and I always imagined you'd be the one to take care of the house in the future."

His words echo my grandmother's in the letter. I do love the house and will do everything in my power to keep it in the family. I pull the letter from my bag. "Speaking of Grandma, this letter was in the box I found. Would you like to read it?"

Grandpa stares at my name on the front of the envelope, written in my grandmother's distinctive cursive, and tears well in his eyes again. "No, that's okay. It's meant for you. I can't...I can't read it right now."

I take the letter back and give him a tissue to wipe his eyes. "I'm sorry. I didn't mean to upset you."

"You're not the one upsetting me. It's just the situation." He looks again at the envelope. "What does it say?"

"It says she hopes I'll care for the house and love it as you have. She mentions something that 'may be of some value,' but I'm not sure what she means by that."

Grandpa's eyes dart from side to side as if looking for something he has lost. Finally, they settle back on me. "Was there a coin?" he asks. "I never knew the whole story, but I heard whisperings about a valuable coin passed down through several generations of women on Winter's mother's side. I got a glimpse of an old gold coin once, but Winter never said anything about it to me directly."

"No, there was no coin. At least I didn't see one, but it could have gotten mixed in with other things or fallen to the bottom. I'll go through the box again."

WE REMAIN outside on the patio, sitting peacefully while we enjoy the panoramic view of the blue waters of Cape Cod Bay melting into the cloudless blue of the sky. The fragrant scent of roses, hydrangeas, and summer azaleas surrounds us.

Suddenly, Grandpa asks, "Where was I?"

"Where were you when?" I ask innocently, although I know he probably wants to get back to his story. I had hoped he would rest.

"In my story. I was telling you about when we bought our house."

"In 1980," I say, helping him to remember.

"That's right. The 80s were tough times, moneywise, but

wonderful in every other way. We worked hard, but our house was our refuge. August came along in 1983, and we thought our family was complete. Then, in 1986, an old store on Route 6A in East Sandwich, just down the road from us, became available to rent. It was a big house that had been remodeled as a store, perfect for our vision. We dug deeper into our pockets, came up with the money for the rent, and the Cape Rocks Emporium was born."

15

SATURDAY, JUNE 21, 1986

Jonathan awoke to a hand gently shaking his shoulder and a soft voice in his ear,

"Wake up, or we will miss the sunrise."

He forced his eyes open, saw the numbers 4:57 displayed on the digital alarm clock, and wondered for a moment where and when he was. Then Winter leaned over and kissed his stubbled cheek, and he sat up to take her into his arms. She pushed him away after a long embrace.

"Come on, we have to see the sunrise today. Let's go."

They walked through the cool morning sand, their toughened feet ignoring the small rocks and shells underfoot. Strands of seaweed lightly circled and fell around their ankles. At the water's edge, they turned toward the east, looking out over the bay. They stood, arms wrapped around each other's waist, and watched the sky put on a display of colors, from orange to pink to golden. The fingernail of the orange sun peeked over the horizon on this first day of summer.

"Thank you, Creator," Winter said softly as the sun became a full glowing circle on the horizon. Jonathan pulled her closer and kissed the side of her face as she continued to look toward the sun.

Over the years, they had often discussed their faith. Winter stuck by her mother's teachings, which mostly followed traditional Native beliefs mixed with Christianity. She occasionally attended services at the Old Indian Meeting House. It was the oldest Native American church in the eastern United States, built to convert the Wampanoag. Although it was a Protestant Church, Native practices were interspersed throughout the services.

Jonathan had quit going to church at the age of seventeen, creating another area of conflict with his parents. The teachings of the Catholic Church, along with its politics, had rubbed him the wrong way, especially once he was old enough to question them. Since Winter had come into his life, he had moved closer to Wampanoag beliefs, but still had a hard time pinpointing what religion he was. He did believe in *something*, rather than *nothing*. When he explained to Winter that he did believe in a source of energy that kept the universe in working order, she exclaimed, "That's the Creator!"

"Well, we've started the day off on the right foot," Jonathan said as they turned their eyes from the brightening sun. "I feel the good luck of the summer solstice pouring into us. This is the perfect day to open the store."

"It is perfect in every way," Winter said. She took his hand as they headed back to the house. It was time to prepare for the grand opening of the Cape Rocks Emporium, the business they had dreamed about since they first met nine years before. Walking along the beach with Winter, Jonathan felt in some ways just like the twenty-year-old kid he'd been back then. But in others, he felt like a completely different person: a grown man who had become a father, who had struggled financially to support his family, while always persevering down the path he had chosen.

THEY PULLED into the parking lot at eight, two hours before the opening. Little April jumped from the side door of the Bronco into Jonathan's waiting arms. Winter unbelted August and swung him down to the graveled lot. They stood for a minute, gazing in awe at the product of their dreams, at the barn-red building with white shutters and a large sign over the door, written in old-fashioned script: *Cape Rocks Emporium.* A large carved bear stood beside the door, holding a *Welcome* sign.

"Uncle Weee!" August cried, spotting Willy coming around from the back of the building. He pulled from Winter's grasp to run into Willy's waiting arms. Willy picked him up and swung him into the air, eliciting delighted shrieks from the almost three-year-old.

"How's my little Indian doing today?" Willy asked, swinging August back down and tousling his straight, black hair. When Jonathan's father had inadvertently first referred to August as *my little Indian,* within earshot of Winter's family, Jonathan had felt like crawling under the table, sure that they would take offense. But when a huge guffaw broke out of Willy, they all joined in the laughter. Willy was the only one who had continued to use the phrase as a term of endearment.

Willy, Mary, and a few other family members had arrived earlier to start setting things up in the backyard. Willy would be putting on a woodcarving demonstration, ably assisted by his little nephew, August. Besides the welcoming bear, for which Jonathan had paid him, Willy had produced many carved figures to stock the store shelves, to be sold on consignment. At thirty-four, Willy had settled into a routine of woodworking, helping out with the Wampanoag Wares business, and doing household chores. He hung out and went drinking with friends on weekends but kept things under control. He dated on occasion but hadn't formed any serious relationships.

Besides the woodcarving exhibit, Mary and her sister Elizabeth would lead a basket-weaving workshop, and a Native dance troupe would perform a special sun dance in honor of the summer solstice. As Jonathan and Winter helped to arrange materials, chairs, and tables throughout the yard, April suddenly called out, "What's my job?" Everyone looked at the serious six-year-old, her silky, brown hair falling to the shoulders of her beaded cotton dress. She bounced up and down impatiently on her little Nike sneakers.

"You can be the runner," Mary said as she walked over to put her hand on her granddaughter's shoulder.

"What's that?" April asked, looking up at Mary, who had not changed much since Jonathan first met her, other than the addition of a few more wrinkles, strands of gray hair, and inches around her midriff.

"You can be the person who runs to get whatever anyone needs. We'll need someone to get pieces of reeds and sticks to make the baskets, and if anyone wants a drink or snack, you can run to get it."

April considered this proposal, her brow knitted in concentration. "Can I run to get a drink or snack if *I* want one?"

Amidst the laughter around her, Mary said soberly, "Of course you can." April accepted the job.

JONATHAN WAS on the second floor of the Emporium, his main responsibility. It housed an open jam space, where musicians could play together, and three small rooms that could be rented for private lessons or practice. Everything was in good shape up here, and it was only nine-thirty, so he picked up his acoustic guitar and strummed a few tunes from the album he planned to record.

For Jonathan, the opening of the store was just the first of two main goals, the second one being, at long last, to record his album. He had been playing with a few local musicians, rearranging and rewriting the songs until he could improve them no more. He had played at a few local coffee shops and community events, practicing the tunes and gauging audience reaction until he felt confident in his own voice.

"Jonathan, your parents are here!" Winter yelled up the stairs.

His parents had promised to arrive before the store opened for a private tour. They visited several times a year, more often in the summer, when they stayed at the house for a few days at a time. The arrival of grandchildren had softened his father's attitude. Although their relationship could not be described as close, as there were still areas of conflict, they had settled into an acceptance of their differences. Jonathan's steady commitment to Winter and his young family had gone far to warm his father's heart.

Jonathan trotted down the stairs to greet them at the front door. He gave his father a quick hug and his mother a long one as he exclaimed, "Welcome to The Cape Rocks Emporium! You get the first official tour of the place!"

"I love it already," his mother said. "It's so colorful and inviting. It's in a perfect place, right on 6A."

Jonathan pointed to the outdoor patio, where small tables and chairs invited customers to sit and enjoy a drink or snack. Inside the front door was the cafe, offering coffee, hot chocolate, juices, and pastries. Winter's cousin Linda was in charge of the cafe. She busily filled the display cases with cinnamon buns, muffins, donuts, and cookies. The aroma of coffee and freshly baked goods scented the air.

"It smells great in here!" Jonathan's father said.

Linda greeted them, holding out a plate of blueberry muffins. After compliments to the baker, they moved into the store's main room, filled with racks of beaded clothing and tables displaying baskets, carved wooden figures, beaded jewelry, and sea glass sculptures. Pamphlets on each table explained the history of Wampanoag Wares.

Mr. Rock picked up a pamphlet and scanned it. "So what's the relationship between Wampanoag Wares and the Cape Rocks Emporium?" he asked.

"We work together based on the consignment model that Wampanoag Wares has always used with other stores. They'll provide us with the goods. We'll sell them and split the profit."

"So you split the difference after subtracting your overhead costs—rent, salaries, advertising?"

Jonathan took a deep breath and glanced at Winter, who gave him an encouraging smile. "Yes," he said patiently. "We've taken that into consideration and have a written contract."

"Good," Mr. Rock replied. "Who keeps track of inventory? Do you have a bookkeeper?"

Jonathan looked up at the ceiling and sighed. "Look, Dad, give us a break. Our doors haven't even opened yet. But we have thought it all through. Winter's family has been doing business this way for years. Between the two of us, we can list what comes in, what goes out, and add and subtract the numbers."

Mrs. Rock put her hand on her husband's shoulder. "Come on, Charles, let them finish showing us around before the store opens. We only have a few minutes."

Mr. Rock lifted his hands in frustration as Winter took Jonathan's hand to calm him. They proceeded into the back room, which held shelves of books about Cape Cod and tables for special displays of local artists' work. The artist on display today was Willy. Several of his best woodcarvings were interspersed with photos of the work in progress.

"He does such beautiful work. His carvings are so life-like and detailed," Mrs. Rock said, picking up a small figure of a chipmunk holding an acorn in its tiny hands. "Is he here today?"

Winter answered, "He's in the backyard. Later today, he will give a woodworking demonstration, and my mom and Aunt Elizabeth will do basket weaving. April and August are their helpers."

"I was wondering where my grandchildren were," said Mr Rock, looking out the back window.

"You can go outside after Jonathan shows you the second floor. I have to get ready to open in two minutes," Winter said.

"Do you need me for anything else?" Jonathan asked.

"No, everything is perfect," Winter answered, giving him a quick hug and kiss.

Jonathan led his parents up the stairs to show them the jam space and the practice rooms. Before his father could start asking questions, Jonathan explained that, for now, the jam space was free for himself and his band members, as they would be the main ones using it. Once they were open and running, he would rent the practice rooms by the hour.

"How are you advertising them?" Mr. Rock asked.

"I have posters up downstairs and at various locations in town. I'm also putting an ad in the local newspaper. My band-mates are talking it up with other musicians they know, and we have a few people interested."

"Well, I wish you good luck," Mr. Rock said earnestly, shaking Jonathan's hand.

"I know you'll do great!" Mrs. Rock chimed in as she hugged Jonathan. "Let's go see those grandkids of ours!"

WITH THE FIRST three hours of the grand opening under their belts, the family gathered for a break outside. A slow but steady influx of customers had increased at noon when the Native troupe performed a summer solstice dance to the beat of a large drum.

They invited onlookers to take turns beating it. Now, with sandwiches from the deli down the street spread out on two picnic tables, they sat down to eat while Linda kept an eye on the store.

April squirmed between Jonathan's parents, giving them a detailed explanation of basket-weaving, while August sat on Willy's lap, playing with a small carving of a dog between small bites of a sandwich.

"What's your dog's name?" Mr. Rock called down to August, who didn't hear him.

Willy repeated the question, and August cried, "Rex!" It was the name of Willy's new German shepherd puppy.

Mr. Rock got up and approached August. "He's a nice dog. Can I pet him?"

August held up the carving for his grandfather to pet.

"Do you want to come sit with Grandma and me?" Mr. Rock asked, holding out his arms toward August.

"No, help Uncle Weee!" the little boy yelled, grasping Willy's shirt.

"That's okay. You can help after lunch," Willy said. "Your grandpa doesn't get to see you as much as I do. Go ahead now." Willy peeled August from his shirt and handed the toddler off to Mr. Rock. August reluctantly allowed his grandfather to take him in his arms.

Two o'clock approached. It was time to get back to work and time for Jonathan's parents to head to the house, where they would stay overnight. Jonathan walked them out to the parking lot. "Thanks for coming and staying so long. We'll see you around six-thirty." His parents had arranged to treat them to dinner at one of their favorite seafood restaurants.

"You're welcome," Mr. Rock said, "It will be nice to have the kids to ourselves tonight. August sure does like his Uncle Willy."

"He does. August has been a positive influence on Willy."

"As long as Willy's a positive influence on August," Mr. Rock said.

Jonathan had never told his parents about the incident with Willy on that first weekend he'd spent with Winter, or about any of the other scuffles Willy got caught up in, but he knew they'd heard rumors. A few years ago, Willy had been involved in another bar fight. This tendency was never far below the surface. Willy did his best to be on good behavior around Jonathan's parents, but his surly side still erupted now and then.

"I think he is," Jonathan said shortly. "I need to get back to work—see you later."

Jonathan turned back toward the store before his father could make any other remarks. Before entering, he paused to take a deep breath and gaze again at the store name on the sign above the door. Its reality soothed him.

The door opened, and Winter came out and stood by his side. "Is everything all right?" she asked.

"No, it's not all right," he said seriously. "It's perfect!"

16

SUNDAY, JUNE 23, 2047

"I stopped by the emporium this morning and talked to Aria," I say as my grandfather pauses to sip some water.

"What a musical name, Aria," he says thoughtfully. "Remind me who she is?"

"She's Linda's granddaughter. Her mom is Julia."

He ponders this until I see light dawn in his eyes. "And her dad is Joseph, I think? He's a nice guy. I remember getting a lecture from Winter once when I innocently described him as Black. I was told that he was Wampanoag before any color. The Mashpee tribe has included many members of African American lineage for a long time. So, how are things at the Emporium?"

"Business is great, according to Aunt April, but operating costs have increased to the point that the profit margin is not what it was in the '30s. I know you had success right after you opened it. Plus, you released your album in... was it 1989?"

"That's right, and 'Waiting for Winter' made it to #40 on the Boston music charts for two weeks in 1990—my big hit! After that, I brought in a little more money playing at local venues on the Cape and in the Boston area."

A wistful smile plays on his lips as his mind wanders back to those times. "The '80s and '90s were good years for us. We all worked hard to make the Emporium a success, and I had my music on the side. I finally took my father's advice and hired a bookkeeper to handle that part of the business. Willy was our master woodcarver, and although he had episodes of slipping back into drinking and drugging, things were mostly okay. Until the later '90s."

Grandpa stops talking and starts to cough. He can't catch his breath. I rub his back, and an aide rushes to help. Finally, he is able to take a sip of water and slowly recover his breath.

"Are you okay?" I ask, still rubbing his back gently.

"Yes, yes, I'm fine," he says impatiently. "Just a little coughing spell."

"I think we should go back to your room. You need to rest your voice."

"That's a good idea. I'll help you," the aide adds.

I WAIT in the hall while the doctor, assisted by Amoon, examines my grandfather. I wonder if I should leave and let him rest, but I'll see what the doctor says.

"How is he?" I ask as the doctor exits Grandpa's room.

"His blood pressure was very low, and his heart rate was fluctuating, but he's stabilizing. He wants to see you."

"Okay, but is it okay for him to talk right now? He's insisting on telling me a long story, and I'm afraid it's weakening him. Should I make him rest?"

"I think you should let him do whatever makes him happiest," the doctor answers.

"Okay, thank you."

Grandpa sits up in bed as Amoon arranges the two deer on

the bedside table. "And now there are two!" she says as I enter the room.

"They were made to go together," I say, pulling up a chair beside the bed.

"I'll let you get back to your visit," she says, placing her hand over my grandfather's. "Take care and rest if you need to. Keep sipping your water."

"I will," he says in a husky voice.

Amoon gathers her things and leaves us alone again.

"Where was I?" Grandpa asks. "I have to finish my story."

"Okay, Grandpa, but please go slowly, talk quietly, and stop if you need a break."

"I will. Where was I?" he repeats.

I sigh and think for a moment. "Somewhere in the 1990s."

"Was your mom born yet?" he asks.

"You haven't mentioned her."

"Well, Soleil made a surprise appearance in 1995. She truly brought the sun into our lives with her bright orange hair and glowing personality. Mary and her sisters proclaimed her to be some sort of goddess. My mother was beside herself that she had a granddaughter with red hair like hers."

"So things were okay with your parents?"

"Other than a few continuing jabs from my father about how I was running the business, things were okay. Everything was falling into place until we hit a few big bumps in the road around the turn of the millennium. I do remember one day just before things got rough. It was April's eighteenth birthday, her *golden birthday* because it was on the eighteenth..."

17

SATURDAY, APRIL 18, 1998

Winter struggled into the kitchen, carrying two large grocery bags, to find Soleil sitting on the table. The child threw handfuls of sprinkles into the air, trying to catch them in her wide-open mouth.

Winter swiftly set the bags on the floor, yelled, "No, Soleil! Stop!" She dashed to grab the toddler. Jonathan came running in.

"Where were you?" Winter asked angrily. "You know you can't leave her alone! She was up on the table. Look at this mess!"

"I just went to the bathroom. I was gone for two minutes. She was in the living room, playing with her toys on the rug. I don't know how she could have gotten in here so fast!"

"Well, by now you should know how fast she is," Winter said, wiping the sprinkles from Soleil's sticky smiling face. Jonathan and Winter surveyed the scene momentarily, looked at each other, and burst out laughing. Jonathan opened his arms wide and took both his wife and daughter into a big bear hug. Winter put Soleil down, and the toddler returned to her jungle of toy animals on the living room rug.

"I guess I shouldn't have left those bowls of sprinkles on the table," Winter said, dismayed but still giggling, "but I need to get a start on the cake decorating. I have so much to do!"

"Don't worry," Jonathan replied. "It's just the usual crew, and we have plenty of time. They're not coming until four." He helped unpack the groceries.

The usual crew was their family of five, Mary, her sisters Elizabeth and Anne, a couple of cousins, and Willy and his girl-friend, Darlene. Jonathan's parents couldn't make it because of a family wedding.

Willy met Darlene at the Emporium when she was visiting her friend, Hannah, their bookkeeper. Darlene was a hair-dresser at a salon in Mashpee Commons. Her own course, dyed blond hair, which clashed with her dark brown eyes and olive skin, always looked like it needed professional attention. She dressed more like a twenty-year-old than the forty-year-old she was and sported a new tattoo every few months. She was known to frequent local bars and had encouraged Willy to join her. Winter and Jonathan hoped those two would both stay sober for the party. This needed to be a special *golden birthday* for their eldest child.

April was a golden girl in many ways. A straight-A student, she had been accepted to Bancroft Business College, of all places. Her grandfather Rock was very proud of her. She had worked at the Cape Rocks Emporium throughout high school and had many ideas for expanding the business. She was also a gifted athlete, playing on the high school soccer and softball teams. With a tall, muscular build, a strong-featured face, and hazel eyes bright with intelligence, she was an attractive young woman. Her long, straight brown hair flowed loosely over her shoulders when it wasn't tied back in a ponytail for sports.

"Is Gina coming?" Jonathan asked. Gina was April's new friend, who had moved to the Cape from New York at the beginning of the school year. She was quite boyish in appearance, with short, curly black hair. Her wardrobe consisted of loose-fitting cargo pants, dark-colored tee shirts, and boys' sneakers. She had come to the house a few times. Both Jonathan and Winter had enjoyed her company, as she was smart, friendly, and funny.

April had plenty of friends but hadn't dated any boys yet. She seemed perfectly happy. Comments and questions from some of Jonathan and Winter's friends didn't initially concern them. After all, it wasn't that unusual for some kids not to date until college. The arrival of Gina on the scene and the frequency of the two girls hanging out together, however, made them begin to question April's sexual preferences.

"Yes, Gina is coming. April asked if we could talk this afternoon when she gets home from softball practice. I think I might know what she wants to tell us."

"Do you think she and Gina are a couple?"

"I think so. After my mother met Gina last week, she told me matter-of-factly that she had suspected for some time that April was a *woman who liked other women.*'"

"Well, if that's the case, then so be it. It's becoming more accepted, and April is strong enough to handle any issues."

"That's true. I think Gina is, too. But I worry about the prejudices they'll face. It's still not accepted everywhere. My mother may be okay with it, but what about your parents?"

Jonathan had no answer to that question, which he pondered as they put the food away and organized the party items. They decorated the cake, allowing Soleil to help, She threw sprinkles in the cake's general direction, then licked off the ones stuck to her hands.

August returned from Mary's house, where he had stayed the night. He worked with his Uncle Willy several hours a week and was becoming a skilled woodcarver. Jonathan and Winter had mixed feelings about this. On the one hand, woodcarving was the only subject that interested August. He had struggled through school. Now in his freshman year of high school, the only subject he liked was woodshop. He didn't even like Gym. April and August were perfect examples of how two siblings could be exact opposites.

Though they supported August's passion for woodworking, they worried about Willy's influence on him. August had already been in trouble at school for smoking pot, and they suspected he drank occasionally. Acquiring alcohol was too easy for underage teens, even with the legal drinking age at twenty-one. They had talked to him about it and warned Willy not to allow August to drink or use drugs when at his house. Lately, however, the regular presence of Darlene had made the situation even more uncomfortable.

August seemed fine today. He was excited about the party and happy to watch his little sister while Jonathan and Winter finished preparations. They arranged shiny, golden birthday hats, plates, napkins, and utensils on the table. Gold balloons sprouted from the backs of chairs, and *Happy Birthday* banners stretched across the walls.

April arrived home a little before two. She couldn't stop exclaiming in delight over the decorations for her party.

"It looks like everything's ready," she said. "Could we go for a walk on the beach before the party?"

Over the years, their beach walks had become the family's best outlet for communication. The waves pounding on the shore and the wind blowing across the sand soothed away every problem.

"We can do that if you'd like. It's your birthday!" Winter said. "Do you want us all to come?"

"Yes, of course," April replied. She glanced at August, who gave her a quick thumbs-up. "And remember, it's not just my birthday—it's my *golden birthday!*"

It was a typical, cool April day on the Cape, but the spring sun felt warm between gusts of wind. The family strolled down the beach, April having chosen to go to the right for this walk. Soleil distracted and entertained them. She ran ahead, got wet when she strayed too close to the water, stayed behind to examine a rock or shell, or asked to be picked up. Finally, Jonathan picked her up and put her on his shoulders.

April took the opportunity to talk. "I have something to tell you. It's kind of hard for me to say for some reason, even though I know you'll be okay with it," she began. "Maybe you guessed it already since I've never had a boyfriend…"

She went on to tell them that she was attracted to girls. She had known since middle school that she was gay. She'd had a couple of relationships, starting in her sophomore year, but hadn't been ready to come out. Gina was more open and didn't believe in hiding anything. She had encouraged April to talk about it. April thought the time was right, especially since she was now eighteen and officially an adult.

"August already knows. He heard the rumors at school, so we talked. He agreed I should tell you before you heard the rumors." April put her arm around her little brother, who had sprouted past her five-foot-eight inches over the last year. He gave her a quick side hug.

Jonathan and Winter took turns giving April their own hugs. Soleil helped from atop her father's shoulders. They assured her that they loved her for who she was and that it was important to them that she could be her true self around them.

Jonathan kept his concerns to himself. *How will Mom and Dad take this news?* Not well, he suspected. Their politics tended to be liberal, but they were products of the socially conservative 1930s and '40s. He was glad they were not here today so that he, Winter, and April could discuss the best way to break the news to them.

The family walked until they came to the long rock jetty marking their turn-around spot. They rested on the rocks. Jonathan and Winter sat on a large boulder a few feet up, and the three children sat below them. August took Soleil onto his lap to keep her from digging in the muddy sand. After a few minutes, a woman with a camera approached. They recognized her as a neighbor from a few houses down. Jonathan called out to her and asked if she would take their picture. It became one of the family's favorites.

The rest of the day went as planned. Gina came wearing a relatively new army camouflage tee shirt. Jonathan and Winter greeted her with warm hugs. She was a very entertaining guest, regaling everyone with funny stories about her family in New York. Winter took her mother aside to tell her about April's revelation, which didn't surprise Mary in the least.

The only downside of the party was that Willy and Darlene did not stay sober. As the evening wore on, their voices got louder and louder. August also looked and acted more relaxed than usual. He danced with his sisters and Gina on the living room rug, laughing and talking with great animation. Jonathan wondered if he had been sneaking something on the side.

Oh well, it's a party, right? Jonathan thought as he watched his family having fun. But a sliver of doubt remained in his mind as he watched Willy and Darlene stumble into the center of the room, almost knocking over a floor lamp, as they joined in the dancing.

18

SUNDAY, JUNE 23, 2047

"I can't believe how hard it was in the past to be gay," I say as my grandfather pauses for a sip of water. "It isn't even an issue anymore. You can date and marry whoever you want now."

"That's still not the case in some countries, but luckily it is here. By the time April and Becca met in the early 2000s, same-sex marriage had become legal. A lot of prejudice remained against gays, some of it pretty harsh. Things have improved steadily over the last twenty years."

"How did your parents take the news?"

"It didn't change their feelings towards April, but they never truly accepted that she was gay. They just didn't and wouldn't talk about it. They were friendly toward Becca, but always a bit distant. They never acknowledged the relationship. Some people are real good at hiding their heads in the sand."

"Wow! Whatever happened to Gina?"

"She and April stayed together for about a year, but April was off Cape at college most of the time. They drifted apart." Grandpa chuckled. "Gina was quite a character, though."

"You said you went through a rough patch at the beginning

of the new millennium. Was that because of what happened with Willy around that time?"

"That was the major incident, but only one of many. The year 2000 hit us like a ton of bricks, even though the world didn't end as some had predicted. August was a junior in high school, barely passing, skipping school, and spending a lot of time at Willy's workshop. Willy was still dating Darlene. We'd heard through the grapevine that she might be involved in dealing drugs.

"We were worried about Willy, but even more about August being around him. Willy would disappear for a few days at a time. We suspected he was using heroin. Heroin on the Cape had been a problem for decades. Something about those bleak, lonely Cape Cod winters drove a lot of folks to addiction, and Willy had always been prone to numbing his anger and unhappiness with whatever substance he could find—drugs or alcohol. Or both."

"I hate to say I understand that to a point," I say, thinking about all those suddenly empty bottles of wine, "but not to the point of using heroin."

"Winter had a feeling he'd used heroin in Vietnam. It was so prevalent there, and his behavior was erratic after he came home. She also knew he used prescription opioids at times.

"Anyway, we tried to limit the amount of time August spent with Willy. But if you tell a teenager to stay away from something, they will turn around and run right toward it. It was a tricky situation. August loved Willy, and woodworking was their mutual passion. We were especially uncomfortable when he stayed overnight at the Jones' house. Mary promised to watch over things for us, but she went to bed before ten. A lot can happen after that.

"We struggled through the year the best we could, keeping an eye on Willy and August and working hard to maintain the business. Production and sales were good, but profits weren't nearly what they should have been. By the end of the year, April was a junior at Bancroft and was planning on using The Cape Rocks business as part of a project to earn her degree. I hoped she could help us determine what was wrong with our profit margin."

"Maybe she can work on that some more now," I say, but my grandfather doesn't respond to this weak attempt at a joke and continues his story.

"We made it through the year 2000, only to get hit even harder in 2001. It was a few days after my birthday, in February. Let's see, how old was I? I can't do math anymore. How old would I have been in 2001 if I was born in 1957?"

"You would have been forty-four," I answer, quickly doing the math.

"That's funny. I thought of myself as getting old then, and I'm still here, more than forty-four years later. Anyway, it was a Sunday. My parents had come for the weekend to celebrate my birthday, so they were still there that morning..."

19

SUNDAY, FEBRUARY 11, 2001

Jonathan and Winter awoke to the sound of the telephone ringing. There was no way either of them would wake up enough to pick it up before the answering machine kicked in. It stopped ringing for a few seconds and started up again.

"It's seven o'clock on Sunday morning," Jonathan groaned. "Who's calling at this hour?"

Winter put her arm out to grab the phone. "Hello? What, Momma?" She sat up in bed. "Calm down. I can't understand what you're saying." She put her hand over her other ear, concentrating on what she was hearing. Jonathan put his arm around her shoulder and leaned close to listen.

"Oh my god, Momma, we'll be right there," Winter said, put the phone down, burst into tears, and fell into Jonathan's arms. He held her while she sobbed into his chest.

"What is it, Winter? What's wrong?"

She pulled back and forced herself to take slow, deep breaths. "It's Willy," she whispered hoarsely between sobs. "He's dead."

"Oh no, Winter!" Jonathan's heart lurched.

"Momma says he died of a heroin overdose. The police just

showed up at Momma's house to tell her. They found his body in his car, parked out near Johns Pond."

She grasped again at him. "Oh my God, Jonathan. He's dead!" She struggled to keep her voice down despite her emotions, to avoid waking the others in the house.

Jonathan cuddled her for several minutes. Tears ran freely down their cheeks, intermingling as he rubbed his face against hers.

"We have to go to Momma," Winter said, sitting up. "We have to go now." She started to get out from under the covers, then stopped and stared at Jonathan. "How will we ever tell August?"

"Let's take one thing at a time. August won't be up until eleven. I'll tell my parents so they can watch Soleil. Dad's probably up already. You get ready while I talk to him."

Jonathan hesitated momentarily before adding, "I'm so sorry, Winter." He wanted to say more, but his emotions choked him. He hugged her tightly, hoping his embrace would give her strength.

He splashed cold water on his face and ran wet hands through his hair, which he had recently cut short. *Willy always kept his hair long*, he thought, still unable to digest the news that Willy was gone. Willy had turned forty-nine in January, and they had joked about throwing a big fiftieth party for him next year. *Oh, shit!*

The sound of drawers and cabinets opening and closing and the smell of coffee filled the air as Jonathan headed to the kitchen. His father sat at the table, reading the Boston Globe, which must have just been delivered.

"Good morning! You're up early," his dad said.

"Unfortunately, it's not a good morning," Jonathan said, keeping his voice low. "We just got some terrible news."

"I'm sorry. What happened?"

"Willy died of a heroin overdose last night. Mary just called a little while ago."

"Oh my god, Jonathan." His dad stared at him in disbelief. "That's awful!"

"I know. There's not much else you can say. Winter and I have got to go to her mother's house. Can you and Mom take care of Soleil? She'll probably wake up soon. And if August comes down before we return, don't say anything. Just call me on my cellphone and tell me he's up. We'll take care of it from there."

Mr. Rock rose from the table, gripped Jonathan's arms, and looked deeply into his eyes. Jonathan noticed the wrinkles and sagging skin of age on his father's face.

"We'll do anything we can to help—just ask," he said.

WHEN THEY ARRIVED AT THE JONES' residence, they found it full of family members, friends, and neighbors lending their support. Women worked in the tiny kitchen, keeping the coffee pot full and placing pastries on plates. Men talked in low voices among themselves. Mary sat on the couch between her sisters, Elizabeth and Anne, quietly sobbing. Anne moved over to allow Winter to sit and embrace her mother. They remained like this for a long time, crying and murmuring words of comfort to one another.

Finally, Jonathan leaned down and put his hand on Mary's shoulder. "I'm so sorry. Winter and I are both here for you," he said. Mary released Winter for a moment to grasp and squeeze his hand, then returned to Winter's arms.

Jonathan looked around the small, crowded house, stuffy and warm with all the packed bodies. The smell of coffee and sugary sweets didn't help. Although he probably could use some of both, since he hadn't had any breakfast, Jonathan felt nauseous.

He reached down to Winter and Mary again and said, "I have to get some air and call my dad. I'm going outside for a while." He made his way through the gathering, nodding greetings to all. All around him, soft voices uttered short tributes: "He was a good guy." "He loved his family." "He was a talented woodworker."

Jonathan walked out of the house into the cold, cloudy day and breathed deeply, hoping to refresh himself. The outside air was better, except for the cigarette smoke wafting around small groups gathered outside to talk about Willy. *I have to get out of here,* Jonathan thought and headed down the street on foot.

He walked with no destination in mind, trying to clear his head. *How can I find the right words to tell August about Willy?* After several minutes, he found himself nearly at The General Store. He had to smile at the mostly good memories the sight of it brought back to him. Besides a new paint job and an updated sign, the store looked the same as it always had. Noah and Molly, now in their seventies, still ran it but were talking about retiring.

Jonathan entered the store, the little bell jingling over his head. Noah stood watching the door as if he had been waiting for Jonathan all morning. The two men embraced silently. When they released each other, tears wet their faces.

Noah finally spoke. "I remember the first time you and I met, right where we're standing now, and I warned you about Willy. You were so young and innocent. I know he wasn't easy to deal with, but I give you credit. You succeeded where many others failed. You truly became his brother."

Jonathan hesitated, trying to rein in the overwhelming emotion that choked him. "Thank you, Noah. We suspected he was using but never found enough proof. I feel sick about this. If only we had done more to help him, to prevent it."

"None of this is your fault, Jonathan. The demons of drugs and alcohol are formidable enemies. They were too strong for Willy to conquer. You must believe, as I do, that Willy is at peace now."

"I hope I can convince my son August of that. He doesn't know about it yet. It's going to devastate him."

"Where is August now?"

"He's still sleeping. My dad is at the house. He'll call me when August gets up, probably around eleven," Jonathan said. He checked his cell phone. "It's almost ten now."

The bell jingled over the door, and a teenage girl entered the store.

"Here's my relief crew now," Noah said, smiling at the girl. "Thanks for coming in early, Carla."

"Of course," she said, and Noah led Jonathan out of the store.

"I'll drive you back to the house," Noah said. "I have to get over there to see Mary. Maybe it will help if I talk to August, too."

"Thank you so much. I'd appreciate that," Jonathan replied. He followed Noah to his truck, admiring the long, thick, grey braid that hung down the older man's back.

JONATHAN'S CELL phone rang at eleven-thirty. His father told him August had gotten up and left the house, headed to his Uncle Willy's. "You told me not to say anything, so I didn't," Mr. Rock said.

Jonathan and Winter waited for August outside the house. When he arrived, his eyes raised in confusion at the sight of so many people milling about. Winter took him into her arms and told him the news. August sobbed inconsolably for several minutes, then broke away. "No, no, I don't believe this!"

he shouted. He pounded his fists on the hood of the nearest car.

Jonathan wrapped his arms around him and tried to pull him away, but August struggled violently. Winter ran into the house for help. Noah came out to help subdue him. Mary followed, leaning on her niece Linda's arm. When he saw his grandmother, August calmed down and slumped in his father's arms.

Mary spoke to August calmly. "I understand you are upset about Willy. We all are. You have not had much experience with grief yet, but it is an important part of life." She held her arms out to August and, wiping tears from his cheeks, drew him to her bosom.

After a moment, they parted, and Mary held August's hand. I need you to help me," she said to him. Then she turned to Noah. "Please help us set up a prayer fire in the backyard near the workshop."

"A prayer fire?" Jonathan asked quietly in Winter's ear.

"It's a fire to honor the deceased," she explained.

She took Jonathan's hand as they followed Noah, Mary, and August to the backyard, accompanied by several others. "It is kept burning until the funeral. That will be on Tuesday. People leave offerings of tobacco or wood in the fire. One person is chosen to be the firekeeper for the entire time. My mother has chosen August."

Mary stopped at a clear area in the backyard, a small distance from both the house and the shed. King, the latest of Willy's German shepherds, came out of the shed to join them. It was evident that the dog was confused about what had happened to his master. After having barked at arrivals earlier, he had retreated to the workshop, where Willy's scent remained strongest.

Mary instructed Noah and August to gather rocks from the edge of the woods to build a firepit. They also collected pieces of wood from the workshop to place in the circle of stones and peeled bark from a paper birch tree to help start the fire. As they worked, Mary explained to August the rules of the prayer fire and the importance of the firekeeper's role.

For the duration, August would stay in the work shed, where he could check on the fire regularly, day and night, to keep it burning. Winter brought out blankets and pillows to pile on the cot that Willy had kept in the shed. When all was in order, Mary led August inside.

The two of them surveyed the walls lined with tools. Carvings in every stage of completion covered the workbench and shelves.

"We have another tradition to follow to honor Willy," Mary said. "We will choose some tools from his trade to bury with him, for him to take into the afterlife."

August helped Mary select a small chisel, a knife, and an awl. They decided to add an unfinished carving for Willy to complete on the other side. After inspecting the pieces on the workbench, they chose an unfinished rabbit, the front half of which was so life-like it appeared to be dashing out of the raw wood.

Then Mary picked up a half-done carving of a seagull from the workbench. She handed it to August. "Willy was so proud that you were following in his footsteps, training and becoming proficient in woodcarving. This is one of the last pieces he worked on," she said. "I give you the job of completing it. Also, this workshop and everything in it is yours. I pronounce you the official woodworker of this family."

August woke in the shed in the dim, cold light of dawn. He pulled the blankets up to his neck for warmth before remembering where he was and why. The night had been a series of intermittent naps between rising to add wood to the prayer fire. He pushed the bedclothes to the floor where King slept. The dog opened one eye to check for trouble, then settled back into sleep.

August stepped into the backyard. His breath clouded around his head as he picked up more wood for the prayer fire. He placed the sticks in the fire, intoning quietly, "I will remember you always. I hope you are at peace now." His grandmother had told him the smoke from the fire would carry his thoughts to Willy. His eyes welled with tears as he stared into the flames.

He looked up at a movement at the edge of the woods. A deer stared at him, the orange glow of the sun rising through the mist reflected in its dark eyes. August stood as still as possible, taking in the animal's regal beauty. Its three-pointed antlers were proudly held above its raised head. August was reminded of his father's wooden deer, the one Willy carved, which had first brought his parents together.

A low growl rose from behind August. He put his hand out toward King to stop the dog from barking. When August looked back, the deer was gone. It had disappeared without a sound into the trees.

20

SUNDAY, JUNE 23, 2047

"Uncle August is such a nice man. He and Aunt Mona always bring a handmade gift when they visit from New Mexico—either a wood carving or piece of pottery," I say, as Grandpa pauses in his story. "It's too bad he lives so far away."

A faraway look lingers in his eyes. "Winter and I were so happy when August finally got together with Mona. I had doubts about using online dating sites, but it sure worked for them. He had always been proud of his Indigenous ancestry and his creative lifestyle, so Mona was a perfect match. He was able to blend into life in the Navajo Nation. Between her talent for making pottery and his for woodworking, they've supported themselves through their art."

Grandpa's voice is getting raspy.

"Are you feeling okay?" I ask. "You've done a lot of talking today. Maybe you should rest now. Besides, I need to leave for Boston soon."

He takes a sip of water. "I'm okay. I want to finish telling you about 2001. It was not a good year. So, let's see, where was I?"

"When Willy died, in February."

Grandpa let out a sigh at the memory. "That's right, just after my birthday. That's why my parents were here. It was the eleventh—February 11, 2001. 'Eleven' was an unlucky number in that unlucky year. First, Willy died. Then came the terrorist attacks of September 11th. That scared the whole country more than you can imagine. Business at the Emporium had been off for a while, but after September 11, it went way downhill. Everybody's business did. No one knew what would happen next, so they were afraid to spend money."

"I've seen videos of those planes flying into the towers in New York City. I can't imagine how frightening that must have been."

"It was terrible and couldn't have happened at a worse time. August took Willy's death very hard. He barely graduated from high school, had no friends, and had no plans for college. He spent most of his time at Willy's old workshop and hid in his room when he was home. His only interest was woodworking.

"We encouraged him in this, and that summer, he began to produce pieces regularly for the Cape Rocks store. He started to make money from the sale of his carvings, and, in September, we hired him to work in the store to earn a little more. His frame of mind improved. Then 9/11 happened, and the world seemed to spin out of control. Three months later, we received a couple more unpleasant surprises…"

21

TUESDAY, DECEMBER 11, 2001

Three months after the terrorist attacks of September 11th, the New York City Fire Department reports that most of the fires underneath the rubble of the World Trade Center have stopped burning. However, occasional hot pockets are still being found.

Winter switched off the TV, poured a cup of coffee, and sat at the kitchen table. Jonathan was due to return from dropping Soleil off at school. She smiled at the thought of her youngest child. Soleil had been this family's only source of positive energy over the past year. Now ten months after Willy's passing, August was still depressed. April was away in her senior year of college, too busy with classes to visit often, but even from a distance, she monitored the Cape Rocks business, which had worsened since the terrorist attacks. She had promised to get back to them soon with her findings on the store's finances.

Winter sighed and smiled wistfully at the memory of Soleil rushing out the door with Jonathan this morning, late as usual. Her never-ending laughter echoed through the house as she pulled her winter hat over her vibrant orange curls. Soleil, so full of life and joy, was always excited to go to school. She was delighted to be learning how to read. She was proud of herself, as were her parents, for always getting perfect scores on her spelling tests.

If only life were that simple, Winter thought. *Oh well, things will get better. This was just a bad year from the start.*

Jonathan thumped up the stairs. She got up to pour him some coffee. A wave of chilly air followed him into the kitchen. He pulled off his coat. From under his hat, his gray-streaked hair poked up in irregular patches around his head. Since he'd had it cut, it didn't seem to know which way to fall.

"You brought the cold in with you," Winter said, handing him his coffee.

"It's not too bad. Soleil was so funny when I dropped her off at school. She told me to have a *pleasant* day. Where did she get that word from?"

"Who knows? She pays attention to everything and has such a good memory. Luckily, the word was *pleasant* and not something else!"

Jonathan laughed and sipped his coffee. "Where's August? I feel like I haven't seen him in a couple of days."

"He stayed over at Momma's last night. I'll call her later. When is he scheduled to work in the store?"

"Not until Thursday." He savored a slow sip. "I don't know what to do about the store. We've always stayed open year-round, but I'm considering closing this year for the winter. Business is so slow. The staff that's left can collect unemployment."

"What will you do for the winter?"

"It's time we updated and reorganized. Also, those few musicians who hang around all winter can still rent the practice space upstairs, so for now, that's still steady income. We can set up paid music events, too. I think this year people need entertainment more than ever."

He smiled slyly. "I can go into Boston and play my guitar in the subway station, with a tin cup."

"Enough of that!" Winter said, slapping his shoulder playfully. "As long as we will be okay."

"We will definitely be okay." he grabbed her hand and pulled her into his arms.

They looked to the basement door at the sound of footsteps coming up the stairs. It opened to reveal a new version of their son. Over the past year, August had let his hair grow down to his shoulders, and he dressed in old jeans, tee shirts, sweatpants, and old sandals or sneakers. This August, however, had short-cropped black hair. He wore crisp chino pants, a button-down striped shirt under a V-neck sweater, and new work boots.

"Good morning," he said, "May I join you?"

Jonathan and Winter glanced at one another, their eyes sharing a silent question.

"Of course," Winter said, greeting her son with a quick hug. "You look so nice. Would you like a glass of orange juice?" August had never taken to coffee, saying it tasted awful.

"I'll have a coffee, please, with cream and sugar."

"Okay," Winter said. She shrugged at Jonathan as August sat at the table.

"So, what's up?" Jonathan asked when they were all seated.

"I have some news that I'm not sure you'll like. You have always said, though, that it's important to make your own choices in life and follow your own path. I'm eighteen years old, officially an adult, even though I can't legally buy a beer yet. I've made a decision that I've thought long and hard about."

August struggled with the words he needed to say. Jonathan and Winter waited patiently for him to collect himself.

"I've joined the army," he said at last. The words rushed out. "I just signed up. I got these new clothes to look good at the recruitment office."

They stared in shock at their son. It was their turn to struggle with words.

Jonathan's shock turned to anger, and he leaped from his chair. "You what?!"

August stood and calmly faced his father. "I joined the army. Please hear me out. I know you're not a fan of the military, but what happened on 9/11 was a direct attack on us. And I need to get away from here, at least for a while."

Winter went to touch August's arm. "Weren't you going to take over for Willy? You have been doing such a good job with the woodcarvings you make for us to sell at the store. I thought you were happy with that."

"I love it and will come back to it, but I still feel lost somehow." He dropped his head and thought for a moment. "Willy served in the army in the Vietnam War. He told me stories about it. Even though a lot of it was horrible, it was an important part of his life. He was never sorry he went."

Jonathan frowned at his son. "Willy was drafted. He didn't join voluntarily."

"That's true," August agreed. "But he accepted the responsibility he was given. He was drafted, but I'm making this my own choice, choosing my own path."

Jonathan turned his eyes away from his son. His anger melted as he listened to his own words come back to haunt him. Now he tried to hide the tears that threatened to fall. Winter put her hand on his shoulder, but he twitched from her touch. "I have to leave," he said and walked out of the room.

August moved as if to follow, but Winter stopped him. She threw her arms around him and held on for dear life.

Twenty minutes later, Jonathan returned to the kitchen and hugged his son. "I'm proud of you for doing what you believe is right, and I support your decision. Please understand; we just don't want you to be hurt."

"I understand that. I don't want to be hurt either!" August said. "I'll be at a US Army base for at least two months before being assigned anywhere else. The army has military posts all over the world, not just in Afghanistan."

"You are going to have to tell Grandma about this," Winter said. "Should we go over there with you?"

"No, I'll talk to her myself," August responded in his new adult tone of voice. "I'll go over after I clean my room and organize my things. The recruiters will contact me soon with the date of my deployment."

ALTHOUGH THE DAY proceeded calmly after August's surprise announcement, Winter found herself puttering aimlessly around the house, trying not to think of her son in combat. Jonathan went over to the store, equally distracted, where he stayed until he picked up Soleil at school.

They settled her at her little desk in the living room, with her afterschool snack and her books. She insisted on doing her homework herself.

The kitchen phone rang. Winter checked the caller ID and answered, "Hello, April!" After a pause, she said, "Sure, I can do that."

Winter called to Jonathan, "April wants to talk to us both on speaker."

Jonathan left Soleil to her work. "Hi, April," he said into the speaker.

"Hello. Dad. Listen, I have something important to tell you."

"You haven't joined the army, have you?"

"What? No, of course not."

"Good!" Jonathan said. "Because your brother did. He told us this morning,"

"What? Are you serious? August joined the army? Mom, is he kidding?

"No, April, he's not kidding. August enlisted," Winter answered in a weary tone.

"Well, good for him! It's probably just what he needs to knock him into shape. Is he there? Can I talk to him?"

"He went over to Grandma's to tell her," Winter replied.

"Okay, I'll call him later. Anyway, sorry to have to tell you this, but I found a big discrepancy in the store accounts."

"What kind of discrepancy?" Jonathan asked.

"There are significant gaps between earnings, expenditures, and profits. They started in late 1998 and continued into the beginning of this year. Someone had to be skimming cash off the top or misreporting consignment sales, to the tune of thousands of dollars a month. It has leveled off now."

There was a pause as Jonathan and Winter took this in. Jonathan put his head in his hands, and Winter covered her mouth with hers.

"How much do you trust that girl Hannah, who does your books?" April asked.

"I don't know," Jonathan said, "but she'll have plenty of questions to answer tomorrow."

"Sorry about this, Dad. Tell me if there's anything else I can do."

"Thank you for all your work, April. I'll get back to you," Jonathan said, hanging up the phone before Winter could say "Goodbye."

"What does this mean?" Winter asked.

"You know what I think it means?" he said brusquely. "I think it means your brother was taking money out of the business to buy drugs. Look at the timing of this—late 1998, after he'd met that woman, Darlene, until early this year, when he died." He paced the room angrily. "Did you notice that Darlene disappeared after that? Supposedly she moved to Boston. She's friends with Hannah. That's how she and Willy met."

"How can you say something like that?" Winter asked. "You have no proof." She backed away from him, holding on to the kitchen counter.

"I bet I'll get proof tomorrow, especially if I threaten to call the police on Hannah. Willy was using heroin, Winter. Do you have any idea how much that costs? Where else would he get the money for it?"

"I am not going to answer that question. You have no right to say these things about my brother when you don't know if they are true."

"Well, I have a good feeling they are. Right now, I don't have anything else to say about your brother. First, our son comes home and says he's joining the army to follow in his uncle's footsteps. Then we find out Willy probably stole thousands of dollars from my company."

"Daddy, why are you yelling at Mommy?" Soleil stood in the doorway of the kitchen, staring wide-eyed at a scene she had never seen before.

Jonathan collapsed into the kitchen chair.

Winter took Soleil's hand. "Daddy doesn't feel well. How about you and me go over to Grandma's for dinner? Daddy will have to sleep on the couch tonight." Winter closed the door firmly behind her.

Jonathan put his head in his hands and let out a primal groan of frustration. The world was falling down around him. The country was at war against terrorists, his business was in trouble, and his family was in conflict. He and Winter had never had more than minor disagreements, which were quickly resolved.

"What am I going to do?" he cried aloud to the empty house.

22

SUNDAY, JUNE 23, 2047

"That was the biggest fight Winter and I ever had and the most depressed I've ever been in my life," Grandpa says. He begins to cough again and can't control it. It's hard for him to get his breath.

I hit the emergency button on the remote, and Amoon and an aide are there in less than a minute. She gives him an injection in his upper chest area, and they massage his chest and back. The coughing subsides and his breathing normalizes. They ease him back onto the pillows and adjust the bed to a more comfortable position.

"He should be okay for a while. You can stay, but he should rest his voice," Amoon says. She and the aide leave the room.

My grandfather's eyes are closed, and he appears to be asleep. I sit in the chair beside his bed. He opens his eyes. They are red and teary from his coughing spell, and perhaps from his memories.

"It's okay, Grandpa. You don't have to tell me anymore."

"I need to finish my story. I feel a lot better. I don't know what they put in those shots, but they work miracles." His voice is a hoarse whisper.

"You're losing your voice. How about if I ask questions, and you answer? Then you won't have to talk as much."

He nods.

"Were Willy and Darlene responsible for the missing money?"

"Yes. It took us a long time to recover. I didn't press charges because of Willy's involvement. But I fired Hannah the next day."

"How long did Grandma stay mad at you?"

"She didn't talk to me until her birthday on December 21st. Ten days later. We came to a truce, but for two years, things remained strained between us, until August came home from the army."

"I remember seeing pictures of him in his uniform. He fought in Afghanistan, didn't he?"

"He did. He didn't suffer any major injuries, but he got hearing loss from exploding shells, and scars on his shoulder from shrapnel."

"It must have been so stressful for you and Grandma when he was over there."

"So stressful that it challenged our marriage. That and the Willy issue."

"Business got better, though, didn't it? By the 2020s, you had two more stores and online shopping. Aunt April has done a great job managing it all."

"She sure has. I wish I could tell you more about the early 2000s, but you're right. I am losing my voice."

"That's okay. I've heard more about those times from my mom, anyway. She loved growing up on the Cape. She's often told me how she felt like an only child, since April and August were so much older and out on their own. I know Uncle August returned to woodcarving and working for the Cape Rocks stores when he came home from the army."

"That's right."

"Mom told me how Aunt April met Becca after graduating college, and they moved to New York City. It must have been tough on her to commute to the Cape as often as she did to manage the stores. At least she could do a lot of the work remotely."

I don't remember as much about my uncle. "When did you say Uncle August met Mona?"

"They met online, sometime in 2020, during the Pandemic." Grandpa shifts a bit to sit up in bed. He sounds a little better. "I think my voice is coming back. I have to tell you a little more about that time." He takes a sip of water.

"Okay, but just a little," I tell him.

"The Pandemic hit us personally right from the start. My mother had moved to her sister's house in New Jersey after my father died. Unfortunately, my mom ended up in a nursing home down there in 2019. She died there in the first wave of the Pandemic in April of 2020.

"2020 was a horrible year—shutdowns of businesses and schools, home lockdowns, quarantines, and fear of the COVID-19 virus, exacerbated by conspiracy theories, political unrest, and an escalation in racial tension. In February of 2021, the family suffered another major loss. It started on my birthday. Don't tell me! I can figure it out. It was my sixty-fourth birthday..."

23

MONDAY, FEBRUARY 8, 2021

"Happy Birthday Grandpa!" Winter called out as Jonathan came down the stairs. "Did you have a good sleep-in?"

Jonathan shuffled into the kitchen, yawning and stretching as he tried to wake himself up. His shaggy, salt-and-pepper hair stuck out all over his head, and a three-day growth of gray stubble covered his face. The rest of him, including his handsome face and muscular frame, was in good shape, besides the natural wrinkles, sags, and a few extra pounds that sixty-four years tend to bring on.

Jonathan smiled. "I think I finally feel old enough to be called that." Their first grandchild was due in March, and they were beyond thrilled. Soleil met Daniel Martinez during her freshman year at the College of Art in Boston. Their relationship built steadily through college. Then, they graduated, married, and moved to Burlington, Vermont, home to a healthy art community. Now, a grandchild was on the way.

Winter hugged Jonathan, sat him at the table with a large mug of coffee, and went to the stove to finish making the big breakfast she had promised him. He had taken the day off to celebrate his birthday and to recover from staying up late Sunday night to watch Super Bowl LV. The New England Patriots hadn't made it this year, but their former quarterback, Tom Brady, with his new team, The Tampa Bay Buccaneers, had won. This added to Jonathan's pre-birthday celebration.

"I hope you're hungry," she said, filling their plates with cheesy scrambled eggs, home fries, toast, bacon, and sausages.

"I'm starving," Jonathan replied, taking a large sip of his coffee, "Not to mention maybe just a bit hungover."

"Only because it's your birthday, I have some Prosecco if you'd like a Mimosa."

"Oh, that sounds great! But I'll eat first and have that for dessert."

"That will be good with my famous homemade blueberry muffins."

"Stop, or I won't have any room for dinner!" Jonathan shouted. They laughed and dug into their breakfasts.

Normally, they would go out for dinner to celebrate a birthday, but things were still far from normal. The COVID-19 virus was still rampant, and many restrictions remained in place. Restaurants could only accept diners at twenty-five percent capacity, to allow at least six feet of space between groups. Face masks were required to be worn at all times when not actually eating. Jonathan and Winter had decided it was easier to get take-out from their favorite Italian restaurant and eat at home in comfort.

Of all the changes the pandemic had caused, eating out was what Jonathan missed most. Although Winter did most of the cooking, she didn't miss it as much. Over the past year, she had done more and more cooking as a way to help the Cape community get through the COVID crisis. Winter, Mary, Aunt Elizabeth, Linda, and others from their crafting group had prepared soups, casseroles, and baked goods to donate to residents in need. The pandemic had affected the employment of thousands of Cape residents, and often, food supplies and household goods at the markets were limited. Although the government had increased unemployment benefits and issued stimulus checks, in many cases, it was not enough.

By this time, over two million people worldwide had died of COVID-19, almost half a million in the United States alone. Most people recovered from the virus, but it hit the older population and those with underlying medical conditions the hardest. Minority populations had also been harder hit than others. The Native Tribal Council of the Cape had developed its own assistance program, which had helped some in Winter's family.

The other good news, although steeped in controversy, was that late in 2020, several pharmaceutical companies had developed vaccines purported to be an effective preventative against the virus. It became available in early 2021, and older people and those with health issues were offered it first. The vaccine was to be administered in stages after that, according to age. Winter wanted to take her mother for the vaccine immediately, but Mary fought it. She didn't trust it and believed it would make her sick. At eighty-nine years old, she was in the most susceptible group to contract the virus. It worried Winter.

Now, Winter tried to keep these troubled thoughts from her mind. She put the muffins and Mimosas on the table for the final stage of their leisurely breakfast, which had turned into brunch.

"Besides eating and drinking," she asked Jonathan playfully, "what else do you want to do for your birthday?"

"I'll need a long walk on the beach after this," he said as he drained the last of his second Mimosa.

"Sounds good to me, but we'll have to bundle up. It's pretty cold and windy out there. Let me clean up first."

"WHICH WAY, left or right? You choose, birthday man."

Winter and Jonathan stood together, looking out over the ocean in front of the house they had lived in for almost forty-three years. It seemed like a long time in some ways; in other ways, it seemed like it was just yesterday when they had exchanged wedding vows, right here on this beach. Those years encompassed much joy and success, mingled with a few doses of sadness and failure.

"Left," Jonathan said, taking Winter's hand. They walked silently for several minutes, their boots clicking over the rocks and sinking into the sand. The cold wind blew into their faces. Thoughts and memories crowded their heads, and each wondered what the other was thinking.

They passed a middle-aged couple walking in the opposite direction, both wearing surgical masks. The couple walked up the beach to pass at a socially acceptable distance of several feet. They did not respond to Jonathan's "Hello."

When the couple was out of earshot, Jonathan said, "I don't get why people feel the need to wear masks outside on an uncrowded beach. I can understand it in town if you're walking close to people on the sidewalk. But it's a bit much here."

Winter took a moment to respond. "It does seem a bit unnecessary out here, but these are strange times. Everyone has to do what they must to feel safe. They may be doing it to show respect for others, to show that they are trying to keep those around them safe as well."

Jonathan put his arm around Winter's shoulder and pulled her toward him in a side hug as they continued to walk. "Of course, you're right. But you know I'm always the Doubting Thomas."

"Oh, sometimes I have doubts too, what with all the issues surrounding COVID. But as you have said many times over the last year, 'Better safe than sorry.'"

They walked along in silence for a while, surrounded by

the sounds of the ocean's gently pounding waves and the wind whistling past their ears. When they came to the inlet where they would turn back, they stopped again to look out to sea.

Winter laid her head against Jonathan's shoulder. "I am so worried about Momma," she said. "I don't know what to do. Instead of choosing to be safe and get vaccinated, she is listening to all the wrong people. I know she's nearing the end of her life, but she is doing well. I am sure she can make it past ninety if she doesn't get this virus."

Mary would turn ninety in October. Winter hoped the Pandemic would be over by then. She wanted to throw a big party and invite everyone they had not been able to see for over a year. The way things were going currently, her hopes were diminishing.

Jonathan wasn't sure what to say about this. He and Winter had some doubts about the vaccine, but had agreed it would be better to get it than not. On the other hand, they couldn't force Mary to get the shot against her will. She was still pretty strong. The vision of holding Mary down while someone stuck a needle in her arm made Jonathan smile, despite the seriousness of the situation.

"You just said that everyone has to do what they can to feel safe. They have to choose for themselves. This is Mary's choice." Jonathan hoped his words would comfort Winter. "It isn't the end of the story yet. Let's research the overall positive effects and try to persuade her that it's best to get vaccinated. Maybe we can tell her she won't be able to see her great-grand-child unless she's vaccinated."

"I've already tried that one," Winter sighed. "Soleil already told Momma that she could see the baby as long as all safety precautions are followed. Some of us have different definitions of 'safety precautions.'"

"Oh, Soleil," Jonathan moaned, taking Winter's hand and

steering her toward home. The wind at their backs pushed them onward.

THEY ARRIVED home refreshed but tired after their long walk. Winter settled down to read in the living room, while Jonathan opted to go upstairs for a nap. It was a peaceful afternoon.

Then the phone rang, startling Winter from her reading. Had she been napping, too? She jumped up to answer the old landline phone, the only one her mother still called. Sure enough, Mary's name and number were on the caller ID.

"Hello, Momma," Winter answered. There was silence on the other end. "Momma, are you okay?" she asked. Deep coughing came from the other end of the line. "Momma, are you there?"

There was shuffling on the other end of the line as Winter waited anxiously. Jonathan came down the stairs, and she gave him a worried look as he entered the living room. She put the receiver near his ear so he could hear the conversation.

"Hello!" she said again into the receiver.

At last, there was an answer. "Winter? It's Aunt Elizabeth. I'm sorry. Mary wanted to tell you herself so that you wouldn't worry too much, but she's in the middle of a coughing fit. She's okay, though. Her breathing isn't bad. It's just the coughing."

"Aunt Elizabeth, tell me. What's wrong?" Winter asked, although she already knew.

Her aunt hesitated before replying. Her voice broke as she said, "It's COVID, Mary has COVID. She was coughing and didn't feel well yesterday, so I took her down to the Urgent Care place to get tested. She didn't want you to know. The results just came back. It was positive.

I'm sorry, Winter," Aunt Elizabeth said, "but I don't know what to do. I'll probably come down with it, too."

"I'll be over there in less than an hour," Winter said, looking toward Jonathan for his agreement. At least he had a good birthday breakfast today, because it looked like there would be no birthday dinner.

"No, you cannot come into this house. You'll get it too!" her aunt cried.

Winter breathed deeply and groped for the steadiest voice she could manage. "I will double-mask myself and bring plenty of wipes and hand sanitizer. There is no way I would leave the two of you alone there. I do not want Momma, or you, to end up in the hospital! That is the worst place of all to be."

"You are such a good girl, Winter," her aunt said through her tears.

This made Winter smile. "This sixty-four-year-old girl thanks you, Aunt Elizabeth. I'll see you soon."

Winter hung up the phone and melted into Jonathan's arms. They both cried a few tears, but just a few. There was too much work to be done.

Winter could tell Jonathan was about to offer to come with her, but she looked into his eyes and told him firmly that he was not to come anywhere near her mother's house. His job would be to get food and supplies, leave them outside, and keep the rest of the family up to date.

"And one more thing, Jonathan. I need you to pray to whoever or whatever you believe in. Pray to that wooden deer if you have to. Just please pray for my mother. This is not the way she should go."

"I will," promised Jonathan.

Winter took one more deep breath and went to pack what she needed, fearful but determined to meet head-on whatever the future held.

24

SATURDAY, FEBRUARY 20, 2021

The family stood around the prayer fire in the backyard of the Jones house. It had been constructed next to the ring of rocks that held Willy's prayer fire twenty years earlier. Unlike then, however, only immediate friends and family had visited the house since Mary's death on Thursday. Now, it was time to put out the fire and head to the cemetery for the funeral.

Winter stepped forward to place one final piece of wood into the crackling flames. "Momma, we miss you, we love you, we wish you peace and happiness in the afterlife, where we look forward to meeting again." Tears coursed down her cheeks, but she imagined the smoke from the prayer fire carrying her words to her mother through the cold winter clouds above them.

She nodded to August, who had once again performed the role of fire-keeper. He poured a large bucket of water slowly over the fire. It sizzled out, and the day immediately felt colder. The smoke curled around the yard as if it didn't know where to go. August poured one more bucketful of water over the fire to ensure it was out. Then the small group headed to their cars, Winter and Jonathan in the lead, August, April, Auntie Anne,

Linda, and a few other cousins followed, all keeping that mandated distance of six feet apart. Aunt Elizabeth looked lonely as she watched them through the front window of the little house. She had contracted the virus right after Mary but was slowly recovering from her bout with it.

The cemetery on the grounds of the Old Indian Meeting House was just a few minutes away. As the cars turned onto the small circular road, Jonathan looked over at Winter. Their eyes met over the surgical masks they wore while in the car together.

"In case I never told you this," he said, "you need to know that you are the strongest woman I have ever known. You've gone through ten horrible days, nursing your mother and aunt without a break, and now you've planned this whole funeral."

Winter sighed deeply, "Thank you, but I had a lot of help from the outside world, thanks mostly to you and August."

"Still, you were the force that kept us moving."

"I wish that force had been strong enough to keep Momma with us."

Around the open grave, located near the edge of the woodlands, about ten onlookers stood scattered at a distance from one another. The minister from the Meeting House stood beside the simple wood coffin on one side of the grave. There would be no indoor ceremony in the small, white-painted square of a building that stood in the center of the cemetery because of COVID-19 restrictions.

Jonathan looked around as the family spread out around the gravesite. He noticed an old man who sat in a folding chair nearby. He was dressed in traditional Native deerskin clothing, with a black feather stuck into his white hair. His long, thick braid reached far down his back.

Noah! Jonathan had not seen him for years. Noah had moved away to live with a cousin after his wife Molly died.

The ceremony opened with the minister intoning a prayer. Then he asked Noah to come forward to speak. The old man rose with some difficulty from the chair but walked steadily forward, the fringes and beads of his clothing flowing around him. He spoke clearly, from memory.

"I knew Mary Jones for eighty years, starting in grammar school. Even as a child, she had a quiet strength, always standing up for kids who had trouble fitting in and helping wherever she could. She was incredibly creative and talented, especially in the arts of beading and weaving. Mary used this talent to build her own family business with her sisters, Elizabeth and Anne, her daughter, Winter, and her son, Willy. She welcomed Winter's husband, Jonathan, into the family with open arms and was blessed with three grandchildren." He glanced at Jonathan and Winter with a twinkle in his eye. "I hear there is a great-grandchild on the way?"

Jonathan and Winter both beamed at him and nodded. Soleil had not been able to travel to the funeral. Besides the virus restrictions, she was eight months pregnant.

Noah smiled broadly, "Congratulations! This is how it should be. One leaves, another comes. The cycle of life goes on. Mary's spirit will continue to watch over her family. I am honored to have known that strong, loving woman."

Once Noah was seated, the minister finished with another prayer and a short sermon, in which he spoke of the cycle of life as Noah had. He blessed the coffin, which, he reminded them, was filled with tools of her trade, samples of her work, and photos of the family to sustain her in the afterlife.

Jonathan and Winter sat on the couch before the living room fireplace, staring into the flames, lost in thought. Winter was back home at last, having spent almost two weeks at her mother's house. Aunt Elizabeth was well enough now to stay alone, and her quarantine would end the next day.

"You must be exhausted," Jonathan said, putting his arms around her. They had dispensed with the surgical masks, as they would now live in their own little bubble at home.

She leaned her head against his. "Exhausted doesn't begin to describe how I feel. I need to go to bed and stay there for a day. I want to stop thinking." She paused for a moment. "I miss her so much."

Jonathan held her as she cried, which brought tears to his eyes as well. He rubbed her back and spoke soothingly until she ran out of tears.

"It was a nice ceremony," Jonathan said. "I was so happy to see Noah."

"Yes, he made it very special."

Jonathan hesitated before bringing up a subject on his mind since the funeral. "I know I've told you that I want to be cremated and scattered over the ocean in front of the house. But you've never told me your wishes. Your tradition is to be buried. Is that what you want? To be buried near your mom and Willy? Not that you're going to die or anything."

Winter sat up and looked deeply into his eyes. "Oh, Jonathan. I am sorry if I never said so out loud, but after you told me about your wishes to be cremated and scattered at sea, I just assumed that we would both do the same. I want to be with you, here, always."

"Always," he said. They looked again into the jumping flames of the fire, into the past, into the future, and into *always*.

25

SUNDAY, JUNE 23, 2047

"The Pandemic must have been very scary to go through," I say as my grandfather pauses. "My mom has told me how difficult it was during those days, to be pregnant and have a baby. She even had to wear a mask when she was delivering me!"

Grandpa's strength has rallied, and his voice is stronger, though raspy. "It was terrible, in many ways. But your birth a month after Mary died brought so much joy and hope to us. We truly felt the *cycle of life* continuing."

"Grandma used to talk to me about that. It makes me feel good to think of myself as part of that cycle. I wish I had met my great-grandmothers, especially Grandma's mom Mary. Sometimes, though, I feel like I know her, because of all the stories I've heard."

"Oh, but you did meet her," Grandpa insists with a happy look, "when you were still inside your mother. Soleil visited once when she was pregnant with you, in the fall, despite the COVID-19 restrictions. Your great-grandmother rubbed a special ointment on Soleil's belly and chanted a Native prayer for a healthy baby. Looks like it worked!"

"That's so nice to hear. No one has ever told me about that before," I say. I imagine the scene my grandfather just described. It makes me feel a closeness to my great-grandmother that I have felt before, even though I never met her. Maybe there was something in that ointment, and in those words she chanted, that have kept our spirits close.

Grandpa continues, "Once the Pandemic was declared over, we had some wonderful times. Those next 20 years, as we grew older, were some of our best, despite all the craziness of the outside world. After we turned 70, Winter and I both semi-retired, although we always remained involved in the business. April continued to run everything remotely. She hired more store managers, increased the online business, which boomed during the Pandemic when nobody could shop at brick-and-mortar stores, and recruited more local artisans to create goods to sell.

"Plus, we had a grandchild to entertain! We loved having you stay with us. We worried you'd get tired of visiting your old grandparents when you became a teenager, but the older you got, the more you seemed to enjoy it."

"That's true. I always looked forward to my Cape Cod trips, even more so when I was old enough to drive down myself. The first long-distance trip that I took on my own was to come here. Plus, I had my own car to drive around the Cape. You and Grandma gave me the freedom to roam. My mom and dad did, too, but I felt more independent down here."

I pause to reflect on those visits to the Cape house with my grandparents and the warm, comfortable glow that always filled me when I was there. Even now, the thought of it fills me. It came from the house itself, so cozy and brimming with love, from the waves hitting the beach and the seagulls calling out overhead. It came from my grandfather: his hugs, his jokes, the silly games we played, the walks on the beach, and the strumming of his guitar.

I take another deep breath and remember where else so much of that warm, comfortable glow came from. It came from my grandmother: our nature walks, the beading and weaving she taught me, our searches for heart rocks on the beach, and the rich aromas of the food she taught me to cook. But mostly, it came from her patience, unconditional love, and understanding.

I look into my grandfather's eyes and see our minds working together now. We both know what the last and final chapter in his story will be. I don't want him to have to go there, to have to talk about the day my grandmother died, but I know he must tell his story all the way to the end.

I rub his hand and say, "I miss Grandma so much. We all do, but I know it must be much harder for you to be without her after all those years together."

Grandpa's eyes mist over as he struggles with his words. "I can't begin to describe what a loss Winter's passing was to me. I just try to remember that I was lucky to have her in my life for almost sixty-five years. I focus on the memories. Those can never die. Even that day started out beautiful..."

26

FRIDAY, MAY 23, 2042

Winter slowly descended the stairs, feeling the weight of the extra pounds she now carried. The heart attack she'd suffered in December had not only ruined the holiday season for the family, it had weakened her more than she was willing to let on. Winter hated for people to worry about her, so she put on a robust and positive front for others, but slowed down and rested when alone.

Hearing Jonathan moving around in the kitchen, she put a smile on her face and a spring in her step as she crossed through the living room. He usually got up now before her, put on the coffee, and started breakfast. That was a sure sign of how their daily routine had changed over the last few months. She decided to make a better effort to get up earlier to prove she was gaining strength. If only she didn't feel so tired all the time, even when first waking up in the morning.

"That smells delicious," she said as she entered the kitchen.

Jonathan smiled and hugged her, "Nothing like the smell of coffee in the morning to start your engine!"

Winter laughed and ran her hands through his thick white hair. "I definitely need something to wake me up! Sorry, I have been such a sleepyhead lately. These days you are always up and busy before me."

He pulled playfully on her thick, gray braids, "You know that's no problem. You've earned it after all those years you were up before me. I want you to get as much rest as you need. How are you feeling?"

"Honestly, I feel fine, other than being tired."

"Well, we'll see Dr. Patel next Wednesday, and you can talk to him about that. In the meantime, keep resting, and let me handle things around here."

Winter smiled on the outside, but inside, she felt like a useless old lady. *Then again, eighty-five is pretty old, so maybe I should just thank the Creator I am still here.*

"I love you, Jonathan Rock," she said, looking affectionately at the face she had loved for almost sixty-five years. Beneath the deep lines and wrinkles, she could easily see the same young man she had met that day at the flea market.

"And I love you, Winter Jones," he replied.

She smiled that enigmatic crooked-tooth smile that had never changed over all these years.

AFTER BREAKFAST, Winter agreed to a walk on the beach, hoping the fresh air would get her moving. The temperature had already climbed to nearly eighty degrees, but the ocean breeze kept them comfortable.

"Right or left?" Jonathan asked as they approached the water's edge.

"I think right this time," Winter replied.

He took her hand in his as they strolled slowly along the shoreline. "It never used to be this warm for Memorial Day weekend. Remember all those cold nights with a fire on the beach, trying to keep warm on what was supposed to be the first weekend of the summer season?"

"Yes, I remember. But the Fourth of July was more like the beginning of the summer when we were kids. Then it moved to the Solstice, then June 1st. Now it seems summer really does start on Memorial Day. Soon, it will be May 1st!"

"They say the climate has leveled off over the past couple of years, so hopefully, it will never be summer all year. I need the winter to remind me how much I love summer, Jonathan said, taking her hand in his. "Although, of course, I love Winter, too!"

They walked hand in hand in silence, listening to the familiar, comforting sound of the waves breaking on the beach and the gulls crying overhead. The rock jetty, marking where they usually turned back, lay in the distance. Jonathan smiled as he recalled April's eighteenth birthday when the neighbor had taken that picture of the whole family sitting on the jetty.

"It will be so nice to see everyone," he said, thinking about what they still needed to prepare for Memorial Day weekend. Soleil, Daniel, and Luna would drive down from Vermont tomorrow. April and Becca would fly in from New York on Sunday morning. They'd see August and Mona at the big family party on the Fourth of July.

"Yes, it will," Winter agreed. She stopped walking and turned to look at the ocean. Jonathan stood with her, resting his arm over her shoulder.

After a few minutes of peaceful reflection, Winter said quietly, "We've had such a good life, haven't we?"

"Of course we have," said Jonathan, pulling her closer. "So far, anyway," he added, facing her.

Winter smiled. "Yes, so far," she said. "I'm tired. I think I need to turn around."

"Of course," he said. He felt a twinge of anger at himself. *I've pushed her too hard.* He eased his pace to match hers and offered his arm for support. She held it all the slow way back home.

By the time they reached the living room, Winter was breathing heavily. Jonathan settled her onto the couch, with plenty of pillows, a large glass of water, and a fan to blow gently on her.

"We ought to call Dr. Patel," Jonathan said. "You seem more tired than usual, and your breathing doesn't sound good. Maybe we should talk to him before he leaves for the weekend."

"No, no. I'm alright. I just overdid it. I'll see him next week. Nothing hurts. I'm just tired." She threw a pillow at him. "Go get the shopping done before all the weekenders get here."

They had made a list of everything they would need for the holiday weekend, including enough food and drink for seven adults. It was strange for Winter to think of Luna as an adult, but she had turned twenty-one in March, just two months ago.

Jonathan was still unsure about leaving Winter. "I don't need to go right now. I can wait and deal with the crowds later."

Winter took his hands in hers and looked into his eyes. "Jonathan, I am okay. I would tell you if I wasn't. Get that shopping done! I feel bad enough that I can't help more, but I promise to rest and be ready for the weekend."

"Well, okay, I'll go. But promise me you'll call if anything goes wrong."

"Of course I will," she assured him. "I just need a nap." She embraced him as strongly as she could manage, to calm his fears.

AFTER JONATHAN LEFT, Winter settled into the couch and closed her eyes. She was so exhausted. At the same time, however, many thoughts raced through her head, preventing sleep. One of those was the box of keepsakes she was collecting for Luna.

She had a sudden desire to check on it to make sure it was complete.

Slowly, she rose from the couch and made her way to the stairs. She pulled herself up, holding tightly to the railing, until she reached the third floor. They had converted half of the attic into an office and workspace. A large desk stood in front of a dormer with a cushioned window seat that overlooked the beach.

Winter opened a box that sat on the desk and looked through the items she had placed in it. She leafed through the old family photo album, and her eyes rested on a thirty-year-old photo of her mother.

Mary had died twenty-one years ago, a month before Luna was born. Winter smiled. Tears came to her eyes as she thought about her mother and her granddaughter, and how they were connected by one's death and the other's birth. She thought also of Soleil, her baby daughter, Luna's mother. It all went round and round—daughter, mother, grandmother, granddaughter, great-grandmother...

Suddenly, Winter found herself dizzy, her knees buckling. She grabbed onto the desk to keep from falling. *I must need to sleep now,* she thought. She repacked the objects in the box and carefully placed the letter to Luna on top. *I feel like I've forgotten something,* she thought. *What can it be?* It wouldn't come to her.

She taped the box shut and wrote *LUNA* on the top with a red marker. Then, she pushed it to the corner of the desk and carefully crept back down the stairs to her bedroom.

Winter couldn't wait to get into that old, comfortable, king-size four-poster bed that she and Jonathan had shared for so many years. As she walked slowly toward it, leaning on the corner of the large, wooden dresser for support, her gaze fell on a figure just a few inches away. How many years ago did that wooden deer, Willy's beautiful carving, bring her and Jonathan together? Winter leaned on the dresser, trying to think, but her mind was not working. She was so tired.

She stumbled toward the bed. *Thank goodness I made it.* She eased herself under the covers. As she drifted off, image after image flashed through her mind: her mother and aunts weaving, Willy carving into a new piece of wood, August looking handsome in his uniform, Soleil's bright, orange hair shining in the sun, Luna's hand in hers as they strolled down the beach looking for heart rocks. And a young man with long, auburn hair, a guitar case over one shoulder, and a duffel bag over the other, his thumb stuck out, looking for a ride...

27

SUNDAY, JUNE 23, 2047

Tears wet my grandfather's cheeks as he finishes the story. I hand him a tissue to wipe them away and pull out another for myself.

"I'm sorry, Grandpa. I wish there were something I could say or do to make you feel better, but I think that's impossible."

Grandpa reaches out his hand to me and smiles through his tears. "That's not true, Luna. Your being here and listening to my long, rambling story means so much to me. Thank you."

"Of course, Grandpa. I love being with you and listening to your stories. I wish I lived closer so I could see you more often." I shift to get up. "I have to get going now, but I have next week off. We'll all be here for the Fourth of July!"

"Really? I didn't realize it was that close. What day is today?"

"It's Sunday, June 23rd. The Fourth is a week from Thursday."

I think about the discussion my mother and Aunt April are having about whether Grandpa should attend the traditional beach party at his house. My mother is all for it, but Aunt April thinks it would be too difficult for him emotionally. They asked me to let them know what I thought after visiting him this weekend. I believe it would be cruel not to let him see his house for what may be the last time.

Amoon enters the room as I gather my things. "I am just checking in to see how your grandfather is doing. It will be time for dinner soon."

"Okay, I'm leaving in a few minutes," I say.

Amoon smiles. "That's okay. I will give you some time to say goodbye and return when you are gone."

I thank her and turn back to Grandpa. "I'll see you next week," I say, gently placing my hand over his, which rests again on the deer. "Thank you, Grandpa, for telling me your story. It means a lot to me."

I lean over and kiss his dry cheek. He reaches out his hand and places it on the side of my face, holding my eyes in his gaze. His eyes have a faraway, cloudy look. "It means a lot to me, too, Luna. I love you more than words can tell."

"I love you, too, Grandpa." I put my hands around his stooped shoulders for a long and tender hug.

"Okay. Now get going before too many of those electric cars go buzzing over the bridge!"

"See you next week!" I say, heading toward the door.

"Wait, Luna! One more thing!"

"What is it, Grandpa?"

"The deer. I want you to have the deer," he says, holding the wooden deer out to me.

"Oh no, I can't take the deer. It's way too important to you! You would miss it too much and be sorry you gave it to me. And I have the doe."

"That's right. But they are meant to be together. I'll be happy knowing they are with you. Let them remind you that you can make changes in your life, that it's up to you and no one else to follow your path and live life on your terms. Please, take it."

I reach hesitantly and take the deer.

"Thank you, Grandpa," I say, almost in a whisper. I wish I could say more words, but they don't come.

MY DRIVE HOME from the Cape is a blur. Images from my grandfather's story crowd my mind, and I cannot rid myself of a deep sense of sadness. I glance at the passenger seat, where the wooden deer leans against my bag. Tears come to my eyes, making the drive even more blurry.

Finally, I make it to Boston, to my apartment in an old building from the 1960s. It's after seven-thirty, I haven't eaten dinner, and I'm too exhausted to be hungry. It takes two trips to bring my bags and the box up the stairs to my third-floor apartment, where I open all the windows to the warm summer air.

Typically, I would pour a glass of wine to help me relax. *Maybe just one?* I think. I remember how many times over the last year I've said "just one" to no avail. One glass always led to two, which usually led to three or more. I get myself a seltzer instead and sit down to look over the items in the box again.

I remove every treasured memento and spread them on my kitchen table. I search carefully through the folds of the box, hoping to find the mysterious coin Grandpa had mentioned. It does not materialize.

I look through the old family photo album and match the people in the photographs with the stories I've just heard. I see my great-grandmother working on crafts with her two sisters. Willy stares unsmiling into the camera lens. April, August, and my mom appear at various stages of their lives. My grandparents sit on the front steps of their house.

I reread my grandmother's letter until my eyes cloud with tears. Finally, I climb into bed, yearning for sleep, but my mind continues to race over the events of the last two days. At last, exhaustion wins out over my racing thoughts, and I fall asleep.

I HAD A DREAM THAT NIGHT.

I was in a car, racing to get to the Cape. Grandma had called, saying I had to get there fast. It had something to do with Grandpa, although I wasn't sure exactly what the problem was. I was filled with anxiety and an overwhelming need to get there, and it was taking a dreamlike, impossible amount of time.

At some point, I realized I was driving an old-fashioned car from the 1900s. The gas-powered engine growled as I pushed the gas pedal. I was obsessed with checking the speedometer and keeping my speed exactly eight miles over the speed limit, sure in my mind that I wouldn't get pulled over for driving at this rate.

Eventually, I knew I was on Cape Cod. Familiar scrubby pine trees rushed by on each side of the road. I rechecked the speedometer to make sure I kept to my optimum safe speed. When I looked up, a giant wooden deer stood in the road right in front of my car. A buck with three-pointed antlers stared into my eyes as I slammed on the brakes.

That moment lasted forever as I held my foot on the brake, knowing there was no way I could stop in time to avoid hitting the deer. I closed my eyes, awaiting the impact. When the car stopped without hitting anything, I opened my eyes to see that the deer was still there, but it had changed.

Now, it was a live deer, not wooden, larger than average. It still looked at me with large, peaceful eyes. On its back, riding the deer like a horse, were two people: a young man in front, with a young woman in back, holding him around the waist. They both had long, flowing hair and wore beaded cotton clothing. Like the deer, they gazed into my eyes. Before I could take it all in, they smiled and raised their hands in greeting as the deer bounded into the woods on the other side of the road.

28

FRIDAY, JUNE 28, 2047

What a difference a few days can make in a person's life. My grandfather died Sunday night, shortly after he'd finished telling me his story, the night of my dream. Amoon went in to check on him in the early hours of the morning and thought he was sleeping, until she realized how still he was.

I feel like I haven't breathed since my mom called to tell me the news Monday morning. It threw us immediately into a whirlwind of activity: contacting everyone, planning the cremation and celebration of life for next week, and getting the house ready for the onslaught of guests. All of this while wracked with a barrage of powerful emotions.

My mother and I have been at the house since Tuesday, carefully cleaning and searching every corner for the mysterious coin Grandpa had mentioned, the possible *something of value* Grandma hinted about in her letter. I shared the letter and the contents of the box with my mom. She had never heard anything about a coin. However, Aunt April remembered her mom and grandmother telling a story about a British coin that had been in the family since the time of the Revolutionary War.

So far, our search has turned up nothing, and we have run out of places to look.

Aunt April arrived this morning, and Uncle August and Aunt Mona will meet us at the attorney's office later in the day, where we will learn the contents of my grandfather's will. He had named April the executor. True to her ever-business-like self, she wants to take care of the financial end of things as soon as possible. It's past noon now, and we are all worn down and hungry.

"We need a break. Let's go for lunch at the Oceanview—my treat," April says. Mom and I readily agree.

The Oceanview is aptly named, and we sit at a table on the outside deck to fully enjoy the view on this beautiful summer day. "Grandpa loved this place," I say. "I can't stop thinking about him. I feel happy sitting here looking out at the water, but I feel like I shouldn't feel happy. Does that make any sense?"

"Of course it does," my mom says, "but it's okay to feel happy on a gorgeous day like today. Remember how happy Grandpa would have been if he were here with us, and how he would like you to feel. He wouldn't want you to be sad forever."

The waitress arrives at the table to take our drinks. Aunt April orders a bottle of Pinot Grigio, saying, "That's right. He wanted us to have a celebration of life for him, like we did for our mom, so let's celebrate."

My mom and I exchange glances, and she gives me a quick wink. We have talked a lot over the past few days, the most we've ever spoken as adults. I told her about my dissatisfaction with my job, the impact of my breakup with Rafael, and my drinking. She has been very kind and understanding, making me regret not speaking with her sooner.

I smile and say, "Okay, Aunt April, but just half a glass for me. I get tired if I drink at lunchtime."

"No problem, all the more for me and Soleil," she says with a grin.

Towards the end of our meal, my mom's device buzzes. She glances at the screen and says, "It's the elder home. I'll call them back. They probably have Dad's things ready to be picked up."

We stop by the home after leaving the restaurant. I recognize the aide Marco, whom I met on Sunday when I was here visiting Grandpa. *How is it possible that was only five days ago?* He greets us and offers his condolences, then helps us load the few boxes containing Grandpa's clothing and personal items into the car. He gives us a list of the items and tells us to ask if anything is missing.

The elder home's manager also comes out to speak with us. "By early next week, we'll need to know what you want done with the furniture from Mr. Rock's room," she says. She hands us another list: two bedside tables, a cushioned chair, a coffee table, a large dresser.

I have a sudden thought—the coin! All of those pieces of furniture had been in the house when my grandmother was still alive. I check the list of small items that Marco gave us, but don't see anything about a coin.

"Can we take a look at the furniture?" I ask the manager.

Aunt April raises her eyebrows in surprise, but I see that my mom is on my wavelength. We follow the manager to Grandpa's room.

"I'll leave you to talk privately," the manager says, walking into the hall.

The emptiness of the room makes my heart ache, and I hold back tears. I head for the dresser that stood in my grandparents' bedroom all those years. My mother chooses the bedside tables, and Aunt April picks the coffee table.

"The coin?" she asks, understanding in her eyes.

"This is the only place we haven't looked," I answer.

I pull out the bottom drawers of the dresser. Sometimes things can get stuck in the back of drawers and fall to the bottom. I remove all the drawers and stack them on the floor, but I don't see anything. My mom and aunt don't find anything, either. They come over to help me. We look inside the empty dresser and emit a collective sigh.

"Nothing," I say.

I lean over to examine the interior more closely. Then I see it.

An envelope is taped to the inside top of the dresser. I carefully unpeel it from the wood and hold it up. My mom's and aunt's eyes are wide, their mouths open.

The envelope is addressed to my grandmother. In the corner is the return address of a coin-grading service. I open the envelope and remove an official-looking document folded around a small, heavy object. It is a gold coin bearing the profile of a long-haired, noble-looking man, Latin words encircling his head. Our eyes and mouths open even farther at the number at the bottom of the appraisal sheet.

We are still in shock as we drive to the attorney's office for the reading of the will. April says, "This may change things a little. That appraisal is from seven years ago, so we'll have to get the coin reappraised and add it to the assets. We'll talk to the attorney about it."

April didn't know the exact contents of the will, but we assume my grandfather had split things evenly. The question of selling or renting the house has been laid aside until after the funeral. We arrive at the attorney's office just as Uncle August and Aunt Mona step out of their rented car. I haven't seen them in a few years. Gray hair has replaced most of the black. Hugs are given all around, and we proceed into the office.

The three siblings—April, August, and Soleil—sit on one side of the conference table, in order of age, and Mona and I sit on the other. I can't help thinking about that photograph taken on the beach so long ago, on April's eighteenth birthday.

April is sixty-seven now, still trim and athletic. Many fine lines are carved into her strong face. The older she gets, the more she resembles her mother. She keeps her hair brown, though a little lighter and shorter than it used to be. August will be sixty-four this year. My mom, Soleil, the baby of the family, will be fifty-two in a couple of weeks. She also helps her hair to stay red, although it is a little darker than that bright orange she had as a child. Then I think about the two people missing from the picture and again sadness overwhelms me.

The attorney clears his throat and explains that April has the right as executor to see the contents of the will before everyone else, but she waives this. He then lists the essential points. Ownership of the Cape Rocks Emporium has been passed to April. August and Soleil are beneficiaries of a significant life insurance policy. All three of Grandpa's children will split all remaining assets, except for the house. That has been placed in a trust for his granddaughter, Luna Rock Martinez.

"Could you say that last part again?" I ask incredulously as the room explodes in cheers and applause.

"Mr. Rock put the house in a trust for you as sole beneficiary. He did include special instructions, which state that his three children should continue to have use of the house when desired."

More cheers follow this announcement. I look around the table at my family's excited faces and break down into tears.

29

MONDAY, JULY 8, 2047

Finally, the house—my house—is quiet. My parents were the last to leave yesterday, promising to return soon to help me move out of my apartment. I've told my landlord in Boston I'll be out by the end of the month, and I will meet with my boss on Thursday to give her a two-week notice.

The coin has been reappraised and found to be worth far more than we could have hoped. The family has agreed to sell it and use the money for repairs, upkeep, and property tax on the house for the next few years. I will work part-time at the Cape Rocks Emporium to earn money for my own needs and spend the rest of my time writing, which, hopefully, will also turn into a paying job. Like my grandfather before me, I will make a go of living on old Cape Cod.

The celebration of life for my grandfather, which we held on the Fourth of July, his favorite holiday, was a success. Two days before, in a private ceremony, we scattered his ashes at sea, about a mile out from the house, in the same place we had cast my grandmother's ashes. So, on July 2nd, the seventieth anniversary of their meeting, my grandparents were together once again in the place they most loved, where their spirits will remain. *Always.*

My grandfather would have been proud of the celebration on the Fourth. The weather was as perfect as possible—not raining but lightly overcast to block out some of the sun's ninety-degree rays. Over a hundred people attended at some point during the day-long celebration. The staff from the Cape Rocks Emporium and friends from local restaurants donated, cooked, and served a wide array of food. An Indigenous dance troupe performed, which included several cousins from Grandma's side of the family. A few local musicians played guitar and sang several of Grandpa's songs, including "Waiting for Winter."

Adam Foster, the guy I had met at the party next door, rounded up tables, chairs, and umbrellas. They seemed to materialize out of nowhere. He built a bar out of spare wood he found in the basement of the neighbor's house he was renting. The initial attraction I felt for Adam, back on that Saturday night only two weeks ago— it seems more like two years ago— has grown considerably during these stressful days. He has provided me with unquestioning, understanding support, and we have grown closer than expected in such a short time. He left on Saturday, but we will get together when I'm in Boston on Thursday.

Toward the end of the day, several people stood to share memories of my grandfather, ending with an emotional speech by Uncle August. He stood on the beach in front of the house with his back to the ocean, and spoke through tears about his father.

"Thank you all for coming to share in this Celebration of Life for my father, Jonathan Rock. My father and mother both believed strongly in celebrating life, in making each day joyful. My dad believed in following your path, in making your own choices, in following your dreams. He instilled these beliefs in my sisters and me, allowing us to choose our own paths, even if they did not go in the direction he would have taken. Along with my mom, he built a life from scratch on Cape Cod, barely scraping by for several years before finding success with the Cape Rocks Emporium. My dad also had modest success with his first love, music, with the recording of two albums and his hit song, 'Waiting for Winter.'"

He looked skyward. "Thank you, Dad. Thank you for all you've done for our family and the Cape Cod community. Thanks for all the great memories. And may you and Mom be together, always, in this place you love."

August took a rose from a bouquet on a nearby table, walked to the water's edge, and threw it in. Aunt April and my mom followed suit, as did the rest of the family, until several red roses bobbed in the blue-green waters of Cape Cod Bay.

Now, I sit at the desk in front of the window on the third floor of my grandparents' house—no, wait, my house—which faces the beach and ocean beyond. The windows are open to the warm breeze and soothing sound of the surf breaking on the beach, broken by occasional shouts and laughter from beach walkers.

I look down at the blank notebook on my desk. I have sharpened several pencils, which wait patiently beside the notebook. The same old questions haunt me, as they do whenever I sit down to write: *What will I write about? How do I start? Will it be any good?* The two wooden deer, which I have placed on the corner of the desk, look at me in anticipation.

Then, it comes to me. It's all right there in front of me. My grandfather didn't just leave me his house. He left me his story.

I will write my grandfather's story about living life on your own terms, finding love, raising a family, and sticking it out through good times and bad. I will write about Cape Cod, the deer, the Wampanoag ways, the Cape Rocks Emporium, the house, the beach, and the heart rocks.

"I'll write your story, Grandpa," I say aloud. "And then, I promise you, I'll write my own."

I pick up a pencil and neatly write the title at the top of the page:

Deer in the Road

Waiting for Winter
   -by Nick Sabbag
   (Jonathan's song on page 199)

Got those summertime blues
    Man, do I feel like I've paid my dues
    Fighting the fight
    To live my life
    Through the heat of the sun.

Waiting for Winter
    To calm my soul
    To make me feel
    Like I am whole
    Need to breathe
    That cold, clean air
    To make me feel like I am here.
    Waiting for Winter to come...Whah oh, whah oh...

I've had enough of the heat
    I'm so lowdown and beat
    Need the relief that chill wind can bring
    To my heart and all my...
    Waiting for Winter to come...Whah oh, whah oh...

Winter, oh Winter
    How I love that...
    Cool, soft touch
    That soothes my soul
    Winter, oh Winter, how I love you...

Watch the video of Nick Sabbag's performance of 'Waiting for
Winter' on YouTube at: https://tinyurl.com/waiting-for-winter

A NOTE FROM THE AUTHOR

It is with deep respect for Indigenous culture that I have included Native American characters and culture in this story. Through my research and readings, I have done my best to be as accurate as possible to honor the Mashpee Wampanoag people.

BIBLIOGRAPHY

I used the following resources in my research on Wampanoag traditions:

Mashpee Wampanoag Indian Museum, 414 Main Street, Mashpee, MA, 02649: mashpeewampanoagtribe.nsn.gov>museum

Mashpee Wampanoag Tribe: mashpeewampanoagtribe.nsn.gov

Plimoth Patuxet Museums, 137 Warren Ave, Plymouth, MA, 02360: plimoth.org

Silverman, David J, This Land is Their Land: The Wampanoag Indians, Plymouth Colony, and the Troubled History of Thanksgiving, New York, NY, Bloomsbury Publishing, 2019

ACKNOWLEDGMENTS

I am grateful to Anthony Manupelli and Regina O'Toole for their vision in creating the Writers' Collaborative Learning Center (WCLC) in Reading, Massachusetts. The support, guidance, and encouragement I received there made this book possible.

My heartfelt thanks to Jim Smith, Laura Hatosy, Karin Round, Nancy Parsons, and Anthony T. Manupelli, the members of my critique group, for their insightful comments and suggestions.

Special thanks to Jim Smith for his confidence-building support and faith in this project, as well as his technological skills and knowledge in the field of independent publishing.

I am indebted to Sally M. Chetwynd of Brass Castle Arts, Wakefield, MA, for her superb editing skills and for "polishing my gem."

To my husband, Lew, and all of my family, friends, and fellow writers who have given me useful advice and positive feedback, I am filled with gratitude.

ABOUT THE AUTHOR

Claudette Sabbag is a retired teacher living in Massachusetts. Besides reading and writing, she enjoys golfing, walking, and beaching. She likes to cook, but prefers to eat out. Her family has a condo in Maine, where she enjoys going to watch other people ski. This is Claudette's first novel, the beginning of the next chapter of her life.

Thank you for reading this book. I would greatly appreciate it if you could submit a review to your outlet of purchase or at Goodreads.